ISBN: 978-0-578-76924-0

ACKNOWLEDGMENTS

My thanks to the numerous readers and others who provided me so much help in turning this story into a book worth reading. This long list includes my wife, my sister, the Burlington Writers Workshop, and the St. Albans Library writers group. Thanks to you all and the many others who have provided so much help.

Jim Stiles

Prologue

My strongest memories of the Bad Times are of turmoil and of hunger. I can't remember a time in my life when climate change wasn't an issue. I was still a child when climate change started to really roll in on us. I don't remember life ever being easy, but as things got bad everything just kept getting harder and harder. Life as we had known it was coming apart. Food was scarce. There were incidents back then where people came into our town intent on taking from us and our neighbors. Law and order was no longer something you could count on. My father and mother wouldn't talk about those times, and would never say what happened to those people.

As things continued to get worse, my parents finally decided we had to leave – to go north while it was still possible. The trip was a bad one. I still have nightmares about it. When I wake up from them, what helps most is when my wife comforts me, always repeating the same assurances about how our children have never experienced those things, and how things are getting better.

The trip north was long, and when we finally got to New Hampshire things got better. I remember clearly how relieved my father and mother were to be getting so close to our goal. Then came word of the Closures. At first my parents wouldn't believe the stories – that we would not be permitted to proceed from New Hampshire into Vermont or Canada. We pressed on until we got to Lebanon, NH.

Oddly, I remember that summer in Lebanon as being mostly a good one, at least compared to the years before we left our home to head north. We were rarely hungry, and we were living with people like us – people who shared our hopes and our goals. I remember how many children there were, and many good times with them. They were not the best times of my childhood, but they were far from the worst.

However, over the years I have come to appreciate that they were very hard times for my parents. At first they couldn't believe we were being refused entry into Vermont. I think what made it so hard for them was how the hope they had allowed themselves to feel as we got close had been taken away.

At the end of that long summer, I remember the noise and confusion as the yellow school bus that had recently arrived from Virginia led the way from the camps to the river, and how we followed close behind in our car. My memory of the confrontation between the people in the bus and the officials who tried to stop us from getting into Vermont is still vivid. My nightmares often feature their bodies, dead or dying, lying by the side of the road, still bleeding as we drove by.

As we drove north along the river on the Vermont side toward New Thetford, I remember how the bus and the column of cars that followed it drove slowly, surrounded by angry, frightened people, most of them walking because they had no cars.

And then, as we got close to New Thetford, there was the huge crash and the fire enveloping the school bus, and people in it screaming as they burned. Then came the gunfire and all the people running down the hill at us, yelling and shooting. I remember my parents pulling my sister and me out of the car and telling us to run away to the river and how frightened I was, and how somewhere along the way my sister and I were separated from our parents – how we just kept trying to get to the river like they had told us to do. All this time, the screaming people kept coming, shooting as they drew closer. Blind fear drove us on toward the river.

I remember getting to the river and stopping on the bank. Then, no longer knowing what to do, my sister and I sat down, hugged each other, and cried.

Then the man – a young man – came to the top of the bank and pointed his gun at us. It was the most frightened I have ever been. I was certain my sister and I were going to die – right there, right then. And then the man – more a boy than a man really – lowered his gun and said to the group of us on the bank, "You are prisoners of the Vermont State Militia. Surrender peacefully and we won't hurt you. I promise."

That was the moment. Right then. That was the moment when things changed. When Tom Grady lowered his gun and promised he wouldn't hurt us, I believed him – trusted him. So did the other people there. He was very stern – I still remember how he scowled. But I also remember how he helped us back up the river bank and walked with us back to the road, helping us through brush and weeds and over fallen trees. He said very little as we walked, but he was gentle with us, and kind. As we walked, more good people came and helped us and promised to help us find our parents and not to worry and not to cry. Ever since then, things have been getting better, at least mostly.

As the Resumption of western society continues, things are not the same as I remember when I was young. However that is not entirely a bad thing. In fact, a lot of things are better. They aren't easy. No one knows for certain what we can really hope for. However, now, decades after the Turnaround, things are much better and are still improving.

My name is Milo Edwards, and Vermont has been my home since that terrible time. Thanks to people like Tom, Vermont has become one of the great success stories coming out of the Bad Times, and I find myself profoundly grateful to the Vermonters who were good to their word – to the promise Tom Grady made. This is their story.

Chapter 1

"OK Tom. Time to knock off. Let's hit the road!"

"Be right there, Dad." Being the newest guy on the crew, Tom finished sweeping up the work area and stowed the broom. He grabbed his tool belt and ran out to his father's truck.

His father, leaning against the truck's fender, handed Tom a soft drink and motioned for Tom to join him. Now that it was September and the afternoon was getting on, the heat wasn't quite as bad as it often had been earlier in the summer. The word was that this summer probably wouldn't set a new record for heat the way the last two had. Regardless, if it only wound up being Massachusetts' fourth hottest as was currently expected, it was still more than hot enough for Tom. He was just glad he wasn't in California where the fires were the worst ever and the economy was tanking as several of its cities burned.

The cold sweat on the can felt good against Tom's fingers. He popped the top and hoisted the can to his lips. The sweet, ice cold nectar rolled across his tongue and flowed down his throat. "Ahhh!" The smile that spread across Tom's face was contagious and flickered across Cole Grady's somewhat grizzled face.

They leaned for a while, enjoying the end of a hard week's work, and what for Tom was also the end of a hard summer's work. As he slowly relaxed, Tom pondered the massive truck, a dually crew cab with the big V8. His dad called it his big-ass truck, both because it was so big and because when you looked at it from behind, the fender flares that stuck out around the double tires on each side did kind of look like ass cheeks. Big ones.

The truck wasn't new. It had earned its dings and scratches on a hundred job sites, but it worked fine. Most Sundays it would get its weekly bath and some more bits of the TLC that had kept it running years longer than most contractors' vehicles. Times were hard everywhere, and the extra work Cole put in on maintaining equipment was a big part of the difference between his business, which was mostly doing OK, and those of lots of his competitors. Most of them had nicer vehicles, but they also had bottom lines that were getting thinner every year. A couple of days before, Cole had said it looked like this year was likely going to be the last one for the Johnson Brothers, his long-time competitors. But they drove nice new trucks.

As he leaned against the aging truck, Tom thought about how his father sometimes reminisced about how things used to be easier – how everything was getting so expensive now. Tom had read an article earlier in the week about how it was true – things were getting harder and stuff was more expensive – and how it was mostly caused by rising food prices driving inflation. The cost of repairing weather-related damage to buildings and roads was a big part of it too. It wasn't that anyone was getting rich – it was just that everyone was paying more because bad weather was doing so much damage to crops, houses and everything else people needed.

One good thing about the construction business was that, although there was less new construction and improvement work, there was more weatherization and repair work. And although working in the heat got tough some days, it was lots better in Newburyport than most places, being in northern Massachusetts and close to the ocean. The other thing that helped construction work everywhere was there were fewer rainy days now, although some of the rainstorms did get pretty crazy.

No doubt about it, climate change was a bitch. A cast iron bitch.

"So Tom, I've been thinking."

"Oh, so that wasn't burning tires I smelled?"

Cole smiled and threw a jab at Tom's shoulder. Then he got serious. "Tom, you're a good worker and you use your head for something more than a hat rack. The guys all like you, and I like having you around too. What I'm saying is that, if you want, when you're done with high school, and college too if you want, Grady Construction could become Grady and Son Construction."

Tom looked at his dad and took a long pull from his cold drink. Tom's knitted brows and scowl showed that he was thinking. "Dad, that sounds pretty good. I've been thinking about other stuff too, but that sounds pretty good."

"Good. I'm glad you're thinking about all this stuff, and about options. Lots of kids don't. The world is changing. I figure there will always be something for a smart, hardworking kid like you to support himself with. But you know how it is these days. I wish to hell we had all paid attention to climate change when I was your age. Things would be a lot easier now if we had been smarter then.

Cole shook his head in disgust and scowled. "What a bunch of dumbasses. I guess you gotta figure that somehow we'll sort it all out, but sometimes I worry." He roused himself, pushed off the truck and headed for the driver's seat, tipping his head toward the passenger seat for Tom.

Following his father's lead, Tom pushed off and walked around the truck where he swung the door open and hoisted himself up and in. "I know what you mean, Dad. I'm taking the new climate adaptation course this year. I guess I'll learn something about it. I'm looking forward to it, really."

"Yeah I think I heard you talking to your mom about that course." Cole cranked the truck's engine and it rumbled to life. "I do like this truck, but the new electric rigs look pretty sweet too. I really would like to have one, but they're expensive and gas is still cheap. I wish they'd pass a damn carbon tax. Then the business could justify the investment in a new rig. One way or the other, some day soon I'll have to break down and buy one, but as long as the big-ass truck is reliable and gas stays cheap, it's hard to think about spending that much on a damn truck."

"Dad, have you looked at the new hybrid power packs you can get now? They make buying one a lot cheaper than the all-electric models. And they're set up for a forklift upgrade to the serious power pack so cheapo's like you can upgrade when batteries come down in price."

Cole grinned. "That's Mr. Cheapo to you, sonny boy" but then turned serious. "Speaking of climate change, what do you make of all the people leaving the south and the midwest. And the coastal cities that flood all the time now. You know, the climate migration."

"I dunno. I mean the economy isn't great here, but compared to the way the heat and droughts are messing up agriculture some places and the way some coastal areas flood all the time, it looks pretty good up this way. Did you see the thing in the news about how pissed off Canada is about unemployed Americans sneaking across the border and working illegally?"

"Yeah, I did. I remember like it was yesterday when it used to be that America was all high and mighty about people crossing illegally into the US from Mexico. Just look at us now. It's bad and I just don't see how it goes anyplace good. Damn." The truck's cab grew quiet as the truck rumbled homeward.

A minute later, Cole roused himself from his dark mood. "You got anything going on tonight? It's a big night – your last Friday before you start your senior year."

"I dunno. Nothing special. Just hang out with the guys I guess. See how much trouble we can get into."

"You're a piece of work. You looking forward to running?"

"Yeah, I think I'm gonna have a good year."

"Well you've been working on it, I'll give you that. And last year you weren't too shabby for that matter, as I recall."

"Yeah, I guess. I should'a done better."

"You gave old Georgie a run for the money, and I think you said he got a cross country scholarship from Syracuse."

"Yeah, I guess. But I should'a done better."

"Ya' know, I got it right the first time – you're a piece of work." Cole smiled.

The next morning Tom got up early and went for a run. He decided to do the paths through Maudslay. It was a mile and something on the roads to get there. A good thrash through the state park's paths and getting back home again made for a long run, but he figured if he was serious about his last season in Newburyport, pushing it a little was a good thing.

Tom decided to push it a little even before he got to the park, so he was sweating and breathing hard by the time he got half way there. As he made his way through Newburyport's neighborhoods, he thought about how his dad talked about the real world – how it wasn't all smooth road and how life threw all kinds of obstacles in your way. Tom thought to himself that maybe that was why he liked cross country running – how it was 'real world' running. Footing could be treacherous. A pile of leaves could hide a rock or a hole. You had to use your head to find a good path for yourself at the same time you were pushing yourself hard.

The run was a tough one. Tom's muscles burned as he returned up the street to the house, satisfied. After a shower he grabbed breakfast. Before he could escape, Cole shanghaied him to help out with a couple of projects, but ultimately was merciful. By mid morning he joined a group of his friends for swimming and a bunch of whatever.

The end-of-summer party that night, although fun, was mostly pretty ordinary. The difference for Tom was the time he spent talking with Elaine Inouye, the smartest kid in the senior class. Although he had always liked Elaine well enough, to Tom's surprise, he found he really liked talking with her. Afterward he couldn't really have said what they talked about. All he remembered was that all of a sudden it was late and he had to go so he could get up for a morning run. When they said their good byes as he headed out, Elaine smiled, and it was like it lit a light inside him.

Chapter 2

As he was heading up the stairs to the high school front door on Tuesday, the thing that was on Tom's mind was his conversation with Elaine Inoue at the party. He had always kind of liked her, even though she was so smart that sometimes it was sort of spooky. Tom knew that he was no dummy. His grades were good and he had better than solid SATs, but Elaine was on a different level. However as they had talked, what had struck him more was how easy she was to talk to. And the more they had talked, the more he had become aware of how attractive she was.

Second period was the first meeting of Climate Change Adaptation. Tom was distracted by more thoughts about Elaine as he walked into the classroom, where he almost bumped into her. As he became aware of her a strange sensation swept over him. It was a little disorienting – like he was waking from a nice dream and transitioning straight into another, nicer one. "Oh, Elaine. Hi. I, uh, forgot you were in this class."

She smiled at him. "Hi Tom. Yeah, I've really been looking forward to it. I think it's really important stuff." Tom stood there for a moment, transfixed by her smile and her beautiful eyes – brown, laced with blue. So beautiful.

It took Tom a half second to realize that he couldn't just stand there and look at her – that it was his turn to talk. He caught his breath. "Uh, I guess so. I mean, I know it's important, but it all seems like it isn't exactly real. No, that's wrong. It's just like it seems like the world should be OK, and it's just weird that it isn't."

"Yeah, I know what you mean. It got a lot more real for me when I visited my aunt in Vermont this summer. She's really involved in the New Thetford project there."

"No shit! Uh, sorry, but that's amazing! Building a whole new town to be super efficient all the way from the buildings they live in to having their farm fields right up to the edge of the town, all so they can walk everywhere. No cars needed, at least for most stuff. Very cool."

"Yeah. It was really exciting to be helping out. All the farms that are part of it are getting ready this year for when construction starts next year. They're also cutting trees and milling lumber in preparation. And, you know, when people get together they all talk about radically efficient this, systemically efficient that, and systemic efficiency the other thing."

"Yeah that's it, radical efficiency. You got to work with…" was as far as Tom got when Mr. Rodriguez interrupted to get the class started. Tom and Elaine grabbed seats next to each other.

Mr. Rodriguez didn't waste any time. He briefly explained that they were going to form teams to do class projects, and how the main focus for each team would be to design a radically efficient community. When he asked them to form up teams of between five and seven people, Tom and Elaine looked at each other, smiled, and nodded agreement.

It was maybe two minutes later that Elaine, Tom, Geoff, Olivia, Izzy, and Mace went up to let Mr. Rodriguez know they were a team. He handed them a piece of paper entitled 'Climate Adaptation Teams' with a list of acceptable team names on it. "Please pick a name."

They looked at each other. Elaine suggested, "Carbon?"

The others shrugged, and nodded agreement.

"Carbon it is. Reading materials and references are posted on the class web pages. The schedule is there too. Any questions?" They kind of looked at each other again, shrugged, and shook their heads. "OK then, next! Come on people we have work to do. Terrie, you and your group come on over. The rest of you, finish up."

Team Carbon headed to a remote corner and claimed a table. As they started talking it was very different from most classes. Everyone's interest was obvious. They were all in touch with the idea of radical efficiency and excited about its significance and potential. When Tom mentioned that Elaine had spent time at New Thetford over the summer, they were all blown away.

As the new team coalesced, they decided that each person should take on one or two focus areas to dig into. Elaine was first to speak up about her interests in farming and soil health issues. Tom was next with his interest in construction issues, which everyone thought was great, given his work with his dad. Olivia and Geoff were into ultralight rail as an alternative to cars, and Mace signed on to help Tom with construction and to work on community layout issues. Izzy took the open space lead and also wanted to help Elaine on farming.

When the end of class rolled around, Geoff was talking about the latest developments in ultralight rail. His passion was contagious. "It looks like the ultralight rail vehicles are really coming together. I mean, they're still conversions from regular cars and some vans mostly at this point. A few big trucks too. But it looks like all the car companies are in and are teaming up with some of the start ups."

Her eyes alight with interest, Olivia piped in, "General Motors has that school bus they're working on with Ultralight Green."

"Yeah Liv, that's right, I forgot about that one. The guys at Ultralight Green do great stuff. Anyway, there are lots of excellent vehicles out there, and it looks like the big car companies are taking it seriously. There are lots of rumors about 'from the rails up' fresh designs for some cars in the works – a lot lighter and simpler than the conversion vehicles they have running around now. Now they just have to standardize on new rail infrastructure. Then we'll really be on our way to real, practical, radically efficient transportation."

Geoff's comment was punctuated by the end of class chime. Olivia and Geoff continued their conversation as people stowed their computers and headed out. Tom and Elaine lagged behind.

Again Tom found himself drawn into Elaine's eyes. "Man, this was great today. I'm really looking forward to this class." As they lingered and talked, the thing that struck Tom was how clogged up his brain felt. For that matter, the air seemed like it was a little funny.

"Yeah, me too." Elaine's smile warmed him.

"It was good talking with you last Saturday, at the party."

"It was a good party. It was really easy talking with you."

"You too." There was a pause. Dimly aware of the time, Tom continued, "Well I guess I should get to class."

"Yeah I guess. See you later." Elaine smiled again and Tom's world got brighter.

Chapter 3

The next day in the climate adaptation class a happy, electric buzz grew as students arrived. They migrated to their seats naturally, eager for class to start.

When the chime for start of class sounded, Mr. Rodriguez headed to the front of the class. By the time he turned and looked up, alert faces and an eager silence greeted him.

"OK. So today we are going to talk about the politics of climate change. As you probably realize, the politics of climate change can get really complicated. We're going to dive in head first, so hold on to your hats." He paused for effect. "Why does the census matter to the politics of climate change?"

The initial reaction to the question was confusion. However their interest was piqued by what seemed like an odd question. Several students threw out ideas. When none of them satisfied Mr. Rodriguez, he narrowed the question. "OK then, why does the census especially matter to presidential elections?"

More ideas were floated, but still a real answer proved elusive.

"OK, a hint. How are the number of seats in the House allocated among states?"

That did it. Mace jumped in with, "The census matters because, as climate change gets worse, people will migrate from places with bad weather, you know, like hotter and drier, or maybe lots of floods, to places where climate change isn't as bad."

"That's good Mace. Terrie, you have something too?"

"Yeah. That probably means that states in the South and Midwest where climate change is so bad will lose seats. States in the north, east, and on the west coast will mostly get more seats as climate change gets worse."

"Excellent point. Now we're rolling! Jim, you're next."

"Since presidential electors are allocated to states based on the number of House and Senate members from a state, states with more people get more electors and more influence."

Over the course of the discussion, Mr. Rodriguez introduced complexities. The last one was a doozy, where he suggested that the shifts in the voter base caused by climate migration might wind up benefiting the Republican Party. "I know that sounds crazy, but bear with me. The states that are hit hardest by climate change are mostly Republican. It looks like lots of people involved in agriculture are having a hard time because of heat and drought. A lot of them may have to move elsewhere. In solidly Republican states, this won't have much impact on who gets elected. However thanks to the way seats in the Senate are allocated and the way the Electoral College works, the per capita influence increases in states whose populations decline and declines in states whose populations increase. It all comes down to the details of how it works state by state and district by district, but it isn't hard to imagine the Republican Party might wind up benefiting from climate change."

Elaine piped in. "But that doesn't necessarily mean that climate deniers will gain any influence. Although the radical right is still the strongest faction in the Republican Party – they still tend to dominate the Republican platform – the pro-environmental faction is growing and the radical right is shrinking. I think it's like 80% of Republican women candidates are pro-environment, and Republican women are almost 50% of the Republicans being elected in swing states."

"Bravo, Ms. Inoue. Although your line of reasoning doesn't prove your point, to be fair, mine didn't prove my point either. In the end, it's all very complicated and it all comes down to counting votes."

Chapter 4

All of the other teams were focusing in on Newburyport and how to move it, or maybe a community like it, toward radical efficiency. When Team Carbon started to move in that direction, Izzy spoke out against it. "Why are we wasting time with Newburyport? Newburyport will never be radically efficient. It takes like a half acre per person to raise enough food. I mean, do the math! Where are we going to get that much acreage? And if that isn't enough, we'd have to fight with the historic preservation people to actually make houses and stuff radically efficient. I mean, like, all the old houses are really great – they really are – and it would be bad to mess with them, but maybe that's another reason why we shouldn't put the work in on making Newburyport radically efficient.

"Anyway, real estate is so expensive here, no one would make changes that would probably lower resale value. If we're serious about creating a REC, we need to open it up. And we can't just think about planning for what it's gonna be like a decade or two from now for a radically efficient community. Climate change doesn't even get really bad for like maybe a hundred years. I mean, it's bad now and it's getting worse every year, but we have to think about how we want things to be when we get really old."

Olivia jumped in. "Like Izzie said, there are lots of reasons why we shouldn't focus on Newburyport. What she didn't say is that sea level rise is going to be a huge problem in lots of neighborhoods. Plumbush already floods all the time, and there are lots of problems all along the waterfront. The elevation of Cashman Park is like five feet, and most of the waterfront isn't much more. And you know the elevation of parts of the Common Pasture – pretty much the only farm land left in Newburyport – are less than ten feet. Since no one has figured out how to protect places like Newburyport, it just seems like a bad bet."

That got everyone fired up. They talked about Izzy and Olivia's issues, and it wasn't long before their perspectives prevailed.

This left them with a problem – since Newburyport was not a good candidate for radical efficiency, they had to figure out some place that would be. Tom took the first bite out of the problem. "You know, retrofitting buildings – any buildings, to say nothing of historical buildings – is hard. It's really expensive, and you can't always get good results. My dad has done some pretty good projects around here with deep energy retrofits. He kind of enjoys them because they're interesting, but on the other hand he doesn't like them a lot because they're hard and complicated. He also doesn't like that the results aren't that great when you compare them to something like a new net-zero house or something like that."

The team batted around Tom's points for awhile, but like with Izzy's, it wasn't long before the team agreed with the points Tom had made. Elaine summed it up. "So we know that Newburyport is a bad candidate for radical efficiency, and so are at least most existing towns. So now we know what we aren't going to do. The question is what *are* we going to do?"

Mace picked it up. "You know, I don't think that's even the real question. I mean, sure, there are questions about exactly what we should build, but we have some really good examples of *what* we should build. What they're doing in New Thetford makes a whole lot of sense. Some of the other projects too. But they're mostly pretty similar, really. What I think the real question is *where* we should build it."

Again, it didn't take long to discuss the points Mace had made and agree. As this agreement emerged, ideas started flying.

Olivia got the flow started. "North. We should go north – as far as we can go."

Geoff responded. "It can't be too far or you can't grow things – you know – permafrost. And land should be cheap."

Tom added, "If you're getting up where permafrost could be an issue, probably zoning and maybe building codes wouldn't be too big a problem."

Olivia came up with another issue. "You know if you're close to big bodies of water, it moderates temperatures, but if you're too close, or the bodies of water are too big, they can generate big storms. So the site should be close, but not too close to big water bodies."

They worked on the list for a while. Tom got in the last word before the end of class. "So, what we're saying is that we need to really figure out where will be a good place to be a hundred years from now, which means we should work on finding a place as far north as we can. Wherever it is, it has to be buildable and good for farming. Seems to me that that means Canada. Sure, northern parts of the US will be a lot better than the south. I mean we could like maybe look in northern Vermont, or maybe northern New Hampshire or Maine. We wouldn't have to worry about permafrost there, but things are going to get really crowded in the northern US, and that means expensive. And like everyone's saying, climate change doesn't even get really bad for like a hundred years, or maybe fifty years. And it doesn't end then. Maybe it starts getting better but maybe not. If we're good, we can really start to slow it down and maybe start to reverse it, but we're betting the lives of our families and kids on what we choose, at least until climate change gets better. And they need to be able to make it if things don't go so well. I think that means Canada. Probably up as far as we can go."

Geoff started to respond, but the chime rang for the end of class.

Chapter 5

The next day Mr. Rodriguez took on a different climate change-related issue – wildfires. This was more the kind of discussion the students had expected and they dove in with enthusiasm. Adaptation to fire was a complicated issue, getting into logging and forestry practices, biofuel production, the biology of wildfires, the effects of soil health on hydrologic cycles, and many more.

Pretty soon the discussion seemed like it was winding up. People mostly concluded that it was all really complicated. Sure some areas should probably have controlled burns to reduce the amount of fuel sitting on the ground. That and a few other good management processes seemed to make sense.

Mr. Rodriguez was about to wrap up the discussion when Elaine interjected a new idea. "Well, you know, there's a big problem that has lots to do with climate adaptation generally and with wildfires. Suburbia and our whole whole 'hop in the car and ....' lifestyle. As long as we hop in the car to go and do anything – even buy a newspaper or, like, milk – we're going to have big problems with wildfire damage because we're going to have houses spread out through areas where there're going to be wildfires. And, you know, if we had farms and gardens surrounding a densely-populated community core, wildfires might not be so bad any more. I mean crops can burn up, which is bad, but at least there wouldn't be dead wood piling up, and the soil would probably be moist, and there would be fire breaks and good access into the fields to make fighting a fire easier. You know, radically efficient communities might be a really good way to reduce the wildfire problem."

Joy from the Hybrid Team responded. "Yeah. But you know, land management could help a lot too. Maybe keeping some areas mowed. And I was reading about how to stop houses from burning up in wildfires. Fireproof roofs are the big thing. Fireproof external walls and shutters too. Maybe a row of like super-fireproof houses at the edge of a subdivision could be a really good firebreak."

Nan from MPG continued, "My dad designs fire sprinkler systems and there's a thing called an exposure system that goes on the outside of a building to protect it from fires. That could be part of one of Joy's firebreaks."

The discussion went on for a while. As it wound up, Tom thought to himself about how smart Elaine was and how great that was. Then he got to thinking about how nice she was and how he liked talking with her. And since he was seventeen years old, his thoughts about Elaine didn't end there.

When the discussion was done and project groups reconvened, Elaine asked Geoff if he wanted to start things, since he had been cut off the day before. He did.

"Amos, Quebec. I was thinking about what Tom said about trying to figure out a good place to choose for our REC. I think he's right about going as far up north as we can. I got on Google Earth and poked around and there isn't much north of Amos, Quebec." Tom and Elaine glanced at each other and smiled – they had done the same thing and Amos was one of the places that had jumped out at them too. Geoff continued, "It looks like a decent-sized town and there are some little towns north of it. And I mean really little. It looks like a good area to consider. But I think we should ask Mace. He moved here from Georgia, like maybe a year ago. We talked a little yesterday about this stuff during lunch, but we didn't really finish. Mace, whadda'ya think?"

"Makes a lot of sense to me. I was telling Geoff about leaving Georgia. When I was really little, my family was pretty comfortable and our town was pretty nice. What with all the bad weather now, things aren't so good any more down there. Four times in the last ten years we had to replace our roof and had water damage, and we had it pretty good compared to some folks. There's so much damage most years that the only people doing very well are roofers and remodeling contractors who fix places up after they're damaged. When we came here we had a hard time selling our house and got a lot less than Dad thought we should. And now things are worse down there than they were and it feels like things are maybe getting worse here now. They aren't saying anything yet, but I'm pretty sure my mom and dad are thinking we should have gone farther up north and not settled on the coast. I hope they're thinking that maybe we should move again sooner rather than later. It's not going to get any easier or cheaper."

When Mace finished, the group was quiet for a second. Tom and Elaine looked at each other. Tom nodded to her to suggest she bring up what they had come up with yesterday.

"I agree. Tom and I talked about it a little yesterday and it was funny. The Amos area was one of the places that looked to us like it might be pretty good. There were some others too. I think maybe we should make this a priority. After all, until you figure out where a new community is going to be located, you can't say much about what it should look like."

Agreement in principle came quickly. Satellite images of earth quickly appeared on everyone's laptops and people started scanning around Canada looking for good places to set up new communities. They found lots of interesting places there and in Alaska too. However, people mostly liked Quebec since it was the closest province and had several good options. Before the end of the class people were all liking the Amos, Quebec area. Just to be sure about Amos, everyone took on investigating some other areas for homework to see if they could find other locations that were even better.

As they were heading out after the end of class, Tom took Elaine aside. "This weekend is my last one before cross country meets start. Maybe we could go up to the Amos area, or wherever it is we choose, this weekend and do some scouting."

"Wow, what a great idea! I bet I could talk my dad into driving us in our new minivan. He likes going places and he's been wanting to take a trip in it."

"Your van's a lot better than anything my family has for a trip like this. Do you think it would be cool if we asked the rest of the team along. Does your van fit seven people?"

Elaine laughed. "My dad would say it holds eight people or twelve teenagers. Anyway it can't hurt to ask."

"Great. Give me a call tonight to let me know how it goes." As

Tom looked at Elaine he suddenly had an urge to kiss her, and it seemed like he knew in the back of his head that she wanted him to. The moment passed, leaving him slightly dazed as he headed to his next class.

That evening when Tom's phone rang he was downstairs with his parents, who had already agreed that Tom could go as long as Mr. Inoue was driving. He listened for a second and let out a whoop, and then headed to his room to continue the conversation in private. His parents shared a knowing look.

By Thursday evening the plans for the road trip were set.

Chapter 6

When school let out on Friday, Mr. Inoue was waiting out front and handed the keys to Elaine (who had been approved by all the parents to share driving duties while they were in the US). He gathered up passports as passengers arrived and when Olivia, the last member of the team to arrive, was in, Mr. Inoue jumped into the front passenger seat to stretch out and relax while he could.

Almost four hours later they were pulling off the interstate and stopping at the MacDonalds in Swanton, Vermont. Geoff headed straight to the counter to place everyone's orders while everyone else hit the bathrooms.

A few minutes later, Mr. Inoue, who had gone back out to check on the fast charge for the van, was joined by a herd of teenagers. He took the opportunity to check everyone's passports one last time so there would be no confusion at the border. Ten minutes later he was thanking the Canadian customs official for moving them through quickly.

Six and a half hours after that they were pulling in to a cheap motel on Route 111, having just passed through Val d'Or, Quebec.

That night was a short one because they wanted to make the best possible use of Saturday's daylight hours. Tom had turned out to be the best navigator, so he got shotgun. Although everyone started the day dragging a little due to the short night, it wasn't long before the excitement of what they were doing perked them up. On the way to Amos they reviewed goals and parameters and all that, and were ready to scout by the time they passed through.

They started out by heading north of Amos, to a ghost town named Joutel on the banks of the Harricana River – the northernmost point of the area they were planning to scout. When they crossed the Harricana River, Mr. Inoue parked and they all piled out and formed teams to scout the ghost town. Tom and Elaine headed down to the river bank. The edge of the river had a firm muddy surface and was easy to walk on. As they walked, Tom noticed a flat stone pressed into the surface. Thinking it looked like a good rock to skip, he retrieved it. When he turned it over, there was an interesting pattern and texture on the bottom surface.

"Hey Elaine, look at this." Tom handed her the stone.

"Hey! Wow! This has to be a fairy stone. They're supposed to be pretty common along the Harricana. They're conglomerate rocks that people think were formed under glaciers. Very cool!" She went to hand it back to Tom.

"It's yours. After all, you're the fairy princess."

Elaine blushed and looked up at Tom, smiling. Tom was moving toward Elaine to maybe kiss her when he became aware that Mr. Inoue had followed them and was watching from the end of the bridge. The moment passed.

Elaine followed Tom's gaze and saw her father. "Hi Daddy. Tom found a fairy stone." She held it up for him to see.

He called back, "Very nice. Why don't you come back and help look over the town site?"

"OK." Elaine turned back to Tom. "Thank you, Tom. It's beautiful. I love it. Thank you." She turned to go back, looking over her shoulder at Tom and smiling.

Before long they finished up in Joutel and moved on. They systematically worked their way through areas south and west of Joutel all morning, checking out other promising sites and just generally trying to understand what it was like. Late in the morning they made another stop, this time to take a look at Mont Douamont, located twenty miles south of Joutel.

After everyone was done briefly visiting some shrubby areas, they headed up the rise toward Mont Douamont. As they went up, the land transitioned from good soil and plant cover to lots of exposed rock, a pattern they had noticed elsewhere along the way but could see in detail here. Before long they emerged onto an exposed knoll. From there they could look all around, including the areas they had traveled through that morning, and just a mile and a half to the northeast, the peak of Mont Douamont.

After a minute of everyone just looking around, Mace nicely summarized what everyone was thinking. "Cool!"

They spent a few more minutes looking around and enjoying themselves. Tom had a strong desire to take a run up to the summit of Mont Douamont, but knew they had to move on. Reluctantly he joined the others as they headed back down to the van.

Around noon they ate a packed lunch on the go to maximize their scouting time. Late in the afternoon, they headed back to Amos via a circuitous route to get a little more scouting in.

In Amos they checked in to a motel on the main drag and headed out on foot for dinner. The van had managed a full day of scouting on one charge, but now it was in desperate need of a recharge, much like the road trippers themselves.

The first thing people noticed was that the menu was all in french. The only item Tom recognized was from the breakfast menu – an omelette. However with some help from Izzy and Mace, people soon had their orders sorted out. Over dinner they discussed a plan for a little more scouting the next morning. It was still early when Mr. Inoue led them back to their motel, just a block from the Harricana River.

Everyone else was content to head to their rooms to relax, but Tom suggested to Elaine that maybe they should walk down to the river. Elaine asked her dad, who eyed them both. "You'll be back in an hour."

"Yes Daddy."

He then focused his full attention on Tom. "One hour."

Tom couldn't remember ever having been impaled by a stare like the one Mr. Inoue leveled at him.

"Yes sir."

Elaine and Tom strolled down toward the river. About halfway there, Tom took Elaine's hand. She squeezed his in return. At the river they found a bench in a small park on the bank of the river and sat, holding hands.

"This is really great."

"Yeah. I'm kinda tired, but this is a great trip. I'm glad you thought of it."

Tom turned toward Elaine and looked into her eyes. "I guess what I really meant to say was, you're really great."

"You are too."

Then their world contracted around them and they were kissing.

The rest of their hour was the longest shortest hour of their lives. They talked, and cuddled a little. There was more kissing. Tom couldn't have said what caused him to think of it since he was so preoccupied with other things, but when he looked at the time, they had less than five minutes to curfew. "Oh, we gotta go."

"No way. It's only been ten minutes. Maybe fifteen." He held his phone out to show her. "I guess we have to go." The disappointment in Elaine's voice was clear.

They reluctantly unwound themselves from one another and headed back to the motel. Tom was worried about what Mr. Inoue would say if they were late. Then he had a thought. "I'll race you back?"

"I wouldn't have a chance, Mr. Cross Country Guy."

"I'll run backwards."

"OK then." She pushed Tom, knocking him off balance, and sprinted away.

Tom recovered and headed off in pursuit, running backwards. He could hear that she was increasing her lead, so he gave it everything he had as he chased her up the hill. He was too preoccupied to notice the many puzzled looks followed by amused smiles and several outright laughs they attracted from people driving by.

Slowly Tom started gaining on Elaine. Crossing a street he nearly fell going off the curb and lost a couple of steps, but by the time they were approaching the motel, he was getting close. He could hear Elaine gasping for breath. Although his breathing was OK, his leg muscles were burning fiercely – sprinting backward up a hill was hard. Not wanting to show off, and a bit concerned about what it would look like if he ran into something in the parking lot, he eased off a bit.

"I win!"

When Tom slowed and turned around, Elaine was leaning against the minivan, breathing hard. He smiled. "You cheated."

She gasped, "And you got beaten by a girl."

"I kinda liked it, although I did almost catch you."

Elaine walked over to him. "No almost about it. You caught me."

A kiss seemed imminent until they heard a door open. "Cutting it a little close on your deadline."

They hurriedly separated and Elaine replied, "Hi Daddy. It was really nice down by the river."

"Glad you enjoyed yourselves. It's time to hang it up for the night – we need to get some sleep so we can get an early start."

They all wished each other a good night and under Mr. Inoue's watchful eye headed into their rooms. Tom had wonderful, confusing dreams that night.

Chapter 7

They were up early and after a quick breakfast – Tom had a really nice french canadian omelette – they headed out to loop through an area they had missed the day before. As they cruised, the weather turned odd – very warm and damp, with odd cloud formations.

Tom was still navigating, so Mr. Inoue asked him, "Tom, could you get a weather report on the radio."

"Sure thing, Mr. Inoue."

"Izzy, I think you may have the best French in the car. Mine is awfully rusty. Could you see what you can make of it if Tom can get us a weather report?"

Izzy leaned forward as Tom scanned stations. On the third one she blurted, "Stop. Yeah that sounds like weather. Maybe some kind of alert." She listened for a few more seconds. "I think that's a tornado alert." She had the attention of everyone in the car.

Mace agreed "Yeah, it's a tornado alert, and it sounds like it's pretty serious."

Mr. Inoue pursed his lips in thought for a second. "OK then. We're heading home." He abruptly swung the car back toward Route 111. "Izzy, and Mace – it seems like maybe your French is pretty good too – please see what you can make of weather details. Can anyone get a data connection on a cell phone? No? OK, how about voice service. OK, good. Elaine, could you please call your mother and ask her to get online to get some more info? Thanks honey."

Elaine got her mother on the phone, and as they spoke Mr. Inoue whispered to the others "If you aren't doing anything else, keep an eye open for any disturbances in the air and for any weird looking clouds." That got everyone's attention.

Within a few minutes they were on Route 111 heading south. Although he didn't say anything, Mr. Inoue was bothered by the lack of cover in case they needed it. There were no overpasses to hide under, and few land features that might give some shelter from a tornado.

The word Elaine was getting from her mother was disquieting.

Rough Road

Multiple tornadoes had been sighted north and east of Montreal, including an EF2. The forecast was for more.

They got through Val d'Or without incident and were moving along well, maybe halfway from Val d'Or to Montreal, when Geoff called out, "Hey! I think… uh, yeah, that's a tornado! I dunno, but… Yeah, I think it's headed toward us!"

Mr. Inoue glanced back out the right side of the van and his blood froze. It sure as hell was a tornado. When he looked back up the road again it bent to the left, which seemed like a fine thing – to be moving directly away from the funnel cloud. He pushed his speed higher.

Over the next minute the funnel cloud chased them, almost keeping pace with the van. Mr. Inoue peered forward and saw nothing. He was about to increase his speed again when on the left side of the road he saw a line of motel rooms with a bigger building – maybe a restaurant – at the end of the row. He whipped into the lot and headed for the small gap between the two buildings. He parked tight against the side of the larger building, opposite the end of the row of motel rooms.

Slowly the sky darkened. Thirty seconds later it sounded like a locomotive approaching and the wind built quickly. Light debris filled the air and when it went dark, the light debris was joined by heavier stuff. The van was taking a beating.

Above the roar of the tornado Tom yelled, "DOWN ON THE FLOOR. AWAY FROM THE WINDOWS!"

At that point the van started rocking violently and the noise became overwhelming.

It continued for what seemed like forever. Then abruptly it began to subside. The noise dropped off quickly and the van settled. Debris settled out of the air and the sky brightened.

Mr. Inoue was shaken. "Is everyone OK?" There were some responses but they were vague and unclear.

Tom piped in, "OK, everyone sound off," and reeled off people's names. Every name elicited a response that was basically positive.

Tom looked over to Mr. Inoue. "Do you think it's safe to get out?"

"Honestly Tom, I don't know. Let's give it a minute. What do you think?"

"Sounds fine to me. I can wait."

When they looked around inside the van there was a 2×4 sticking through one of the rear side windows. When he saw that, Mr. Inoue shuddered. "Tom, good call about everyone getting on the floor. Great call." He thought a moment and continued, "Elaine, call your mom and let her know we're all OK."

When he heard Elaine connect and pass the basic message, Mr. Inoue heaved a huge sigh, trying to shake off the shock. "OK, Tom, how about you and I hop out and take a quick look around. Everyone else, please stay inside until we have a look – I wouldn't want everyone to have to get back in quickly if things are still bad."

Outside things still felt unsettled to Mr. Inoue, but he thought it was probably more him than the weather. "Tom, do you see any sign of the tornado?"

Tom looked around again. "Nothing."

"OK, you hang close to the van and I'm going to see what else I can see." He walked out toward the road, away from the building and looked all around. Away to the south he could see a large black blot that seemed to be moving away. Otherwise things seemed OK. However when he turned around and looked to the north he was stunned. Half of the motel units were gone. Simply not there except for lots of debris and some bits of plumbing sticking up out of the cement slab, a few of them spurting water.

He headed back to the car, motioning that it was OK to get out.

"So you all look like you're OK. Any bad bumps or bruises? Check yourselves over. Olivia, you were next to the window that has the 2 by 4 in it. Check yourself carefully. Elaine, would you help her?"

As he looked over the kids, he noticed an odd look on Geoff's face. "Geoff, are you OK?"

Geoff was silent as he nodded yes. A scowl was plastered on his face and he didn't meet Mr. Inouye's eyes.

Mr. Inouye was worried about Geoff as he spoke to the kids. "You should probably all call your families to let them know you're OK and tell them what happened. What you can't see from here is that half of the motel rooms down there are gone. Let's take it slow, but we should see if anyone needs help. Elaine, when you're done helping Olivia would you go out there in the parking lot, behind those guard rails and just keep an eye out. I don't know about tornadoes, but if it comes back or there's another one or whatever, I don't want to be surprised. I'm going to go try to find someone in charge here. Tom, would you head out behind and check around?

"Everyone! Please! Be very careful. The rest of you pair up and maybe go in opposite directions to see if anyone needs help. There's going to be lots of broken glass and dangerous debris, so be very careful. Go slow." He was pleased when he saw that Izzy seemed like she was aware of Geoff's distress and seemed to be taking him in hand.

When Tom turned to head back to the area behind the motel and restaurant, he felt kind of odd. Maybe disoriented was a better word. He couldn't have said exactly since he had never had as dramatic an experience as this. The only thing that was even close was when he had fallen out of his tree house and broken his arm, but this was much stranger than that. He was awfully glad that Mr. Inoue was in charge. What Tom didn't understand was that Mr. Inoue felt at least as odd as Tom and the rest of the group about their close brush with a tornado.

A half hour later things were more settled. They hadn't found anyone who had been hurt. Word from Mr. Inoue when he came back from checking in with the owner of the motel and restaurant was encouraging. After the owner had calmed down enough to think, he was confident there hadn't been anyone in the missing motel units. One woman inside the restaurant had some cuts from flying glass, but nothing serious.

Damage to buildings and most of the cars was massive. One of the customers in the restaurant was a mechanic who agreed to have a look at the van. He gave it a good look over. Before taking it for a quick test drive, he grabbed a chunk of 2×4 from the parking lot and hammered the one sticking through the window back out again. When he returned, he concluded that it seemed OK, with the obvious exceptions. He also suggested they keep their speed well down until a mechanic could give it a careful look. That was if it was even worth it – the body damage on the van was extensive. He guessed it was probably totaled.

Before he left, the mechanic grabbed a roll of duct tape from his car and taped over the hole in the window. As he was finishing up Mr. Inoue sidled over to Tom. "You know, I'm pretty sure that when I came flying in here I parked up pretty close to the building and close to parallel. Before the mechanic took it for a test, the front corner of the van was damaged from hitting the building and I would swear that the back end was five feet away from the wall."

"And the van had moved forward a few feet too. When I got off the floor, my window didn't line up with the window on the building any more."

Unsettled by their observations, Mr. Inoue developed a strong urge to get on with it – to go home. He let everyone know they should all get ready – that they were heading out in a few minutes. Then he called his wife to fill her in some more. After reassuring her that things were OK, he told her about the damage to the van. She was appalled and didn't want them to drive it anywhere. He assured her that he would keep the speed way down. She wasn't happy.

By the time he got off the phone, everyone was ready, so they headed out. The road was rough, with debris of all sorts littering its surface. Several times they had to swing to the edge of the shoulder to get around a tree or other obstacle. Fortunately, before too long it got better and they were able to speed up, at least a little.

A half hour later Elaine got a call from her mom directing her to get her father to a car rental agency on the outskirts of Saint-Jerome. There would be a van waiting for them. When Elaine told her dad, he sighed and smiled.

It was almost midnight when they got to Newburyport, and a little after 12:30 before Mr. Inoue had dropped all the kids off and he and Elaine got home.

Chapter 8

The next day the story of their adventure was the only topic of conversation in school. Tom actually made it to school on time, barely. Everything felt a little weird – a little off – as he went in and made his way around the familiar surroundings of the school. Slowly the out-of-place feeling receded as ordinary school routines re-established the normality that had been briefly but profoundly disrupted the day before.

Tom didn't see any of the others from the road trip until the second period. However the entire team except for Geoff was there for the Climate Adaptation class. The discussion of climate change news ran long that morning. Mr. Rodriguez finally managed to segue from the drama of the tornado to the results of the scouting mission. Although it was less dramatic, the class was interested in what they heard about the area around Amos. From what Team Carbon had figured out, the area was slowly transitioning from forestry to farming, with gold mining still playing a prominent role in the local economy. The team's on-line research indicated that soil tended to be sour with high sand content. The landscape was generally flat. There were lots of farms, especially closer to Amos, and prospects for agriculture looked good.

Although the land in the general area was relatively flat, some higher hills, including Mont Douamont, rose five hundred feet above the surrounding area and were of a size that would easily accommodate a village center if they wanted to follow the model of New Thetford.

As Olivia talked about five hundred foot high hills, Tom's mind roamed back to standing on the rocky knoll next to Mont Douamont. The rough, rocky surface of the knoll and the slope up to the peak filled his imagination. Again he felt a strong desire to run to the summit of the small mountain.

Over the course of the week, things slowly calmed down. Geoff made it into school the next day. When Tom asked him about his absence the day before, Geoff explained, "I didn't really sleep Sunday night. I had nightmares about the tornado."

"Yeah me too, a little."

Geoff scowled as unhappy thoughts swirled through his mind.

"Geoff, you OK?"

Geoff shuddered and blinked before responding."I guess. It's just that I can't get the van shaking and the noise and all that out of my head. It was a little better last night – our doctor gave me some pills and I slept some. He had me talk to the school psychologist yesterday, and later today I'm going to talk to some doctor – a shrink."

"Huh, I guess that's probably why the psychologist called me in yesterday to talk about it. Elaine too."

"Yeah, I guess. I don't even know why it bothers me so much, but when I think about it, it's like I'm in the van again and the tornado is thrashing the shit out of everything." He shuddered again. "The psychologist thought maybe it might help if I wrote about it, but said I should talk about that to the shrink today."

"Yeah, that sounds smart."

Tom was encouraged when Geoff smiled a little in response. "Well I should get to class."

"Yeah, me too." Tom started to turn to go and then turned back to Geoff. "You know Geoff, let me know if I can help or anything. And remember, you've got friends, lots of us."

Geoff brightened a little. "Yeah. Thanks Tom."

The weekend after the road trip, Geoff and Mace wrote an article about their trip and submitted it to the US Climate Action Society. To their delight, it was published and got lots of positive responses. The strong response led USCAS to establish a dedicated thread for more discussion and provide editorial assistance for postings and managing the thread.

Life got even busier for Tom and Elaine. Tom's running was

very successful, and it was looking like he might have a really good season. Tom found that he really liked how Elaine was always there to cheer him on. He developed a killer finishing kick when he focused his attention on her near the finish, which he credited with taking the better part of a second off his times. Mostly when they got together they would work on their REC project or sometimes other homework, but distractions did happen.

On weekends they became inseparable. Mr. Inoue's concern over a romance involving his daughter which had been so apparent in Amos was less conspicuous now. Although he never said so, Tom's level head and timely help had impressed him during the tornado incident. The problem for him now was he sometimes found himself distracted by the trauma of the experience. The thought of what had nearly happened to the other kids and most of all his oldest child, Elaine, was very disturbing for him.

Tom and Elaine often got together at the Inoue house. As Mrs. Inoue got to know Tom and saw how well he treated Elaine, she became very fond of him. And Tom's mom and dad both liked Elaine. Although very busy, life was good.

Chapter 9

The hurricane season that year was astonishingly bad. A few years earlier a new hurricane category – category 6 – starting at sustained wind speeds of 196 miles per hour – had been added to the list of hurricane intensities. That year for the first time a hurricane officially earned the new classification. It rampaged through the Caribbean and, after dropping to a category 4, struck the Gulf coast centered on Mississippi and Alabama. A month later another major hurricane – a category 2 – hit the Florida coast north of Jacksonville and brought north Florida and south Georgia massive flooding. FEMA was sent reeling by these as well as several other smaller hurricanes and tropical storms that came ashore. Members of the Climate Adaptation class led the school's fund raising effort for relief. Olivia and a cadre of other students became quite expert in figuring out where help was needed most, and finding ways to direct funds to them.

Chapter 10

Not to be outdone by their southern cousins, nor'easters started early. Newburyport was hit by three separate storms over a period of five weeks in October and early November. Although wind speeds were not high by hurricane standards, every one of them involved flooding, in part because several other ordinary rainstorms had kept the ground saturated. The amount of rain that fell over a period of a few weeks was unprecedented. However it was the last nor'easter, named Gavin, two weeks before Thanksgiving, that changed Newburyport. Literally.

Given the wet conditions in the region and the expectations for this new storm, emergency authorities had recommended extensive evacuation of the coast and low-lying areas, especially along the Merrimack River. Elaine lived just uphill from Water St. in Newburyport – still within the primary evacuation area. Still shaken by his experience with the tornado, Mr. Inoue was eager to get out. As her parents and siblings worked out a place to stay with friends closer to Boston, Elaine asked if she could stay in Newburyport with Izzy. Her house was up the hill from Low St. between the hospital and the plaza, well above any flooding. She explained that she wanted to work on her Climate Adaptation project with friends. Her parents, not fooled by her excuse, were not happy with the idea, but ultimately agreed.

The Gradys decided to stay. They lived in the west end of town at the crest of a hill overlooking the Artichoke Reservoir and high above any potential flooding. The Grady house was modest, but Cole had worked hard to make it nice. He had even moved a generator that he normally used on job sites to the garage in preparation for Gavin. It was sufficient to handle most of their demand should the need arise.

Elaine had come over early Saturday morning before the storm got serious so that she and Tom could work on Team Carbon's project and they could hang out together.

When Gavin hit, Newburyport was in its cross hairs. Flooding started immediately and continued to get worse as Gavin followed the course of the Merrimack River upstream. As the storm built in the late morning, Cole got a call from his friend Josef who worked in the fire department. The storm was significantly worse than expected and the city was already swamped with calls for assistance, so they were putting out the call for more help. Josef knew that Cole could handle himself and owned every tool known to man. Cole agreed, and immediately went into conference with his wife while Tom and Elaine sat at the dining room table with all their project materials spread out and two computers humming.

When Tom's parents emerged from the kitchen, Tom's mother was silent and clearly not too happy.

Cole approached Tom. "Tom, it's entirely up to you. It could get hairy out there. I guess it's already bad and is going to get worse. Joe says they're looking for all the help they can get. If you want to come along, your mother and I agree that it's OK with us."

Conflicting thoughts hit Tom, but his desire to help, maybe colored by a desire to show off to his girlfriend, decided him. "I'll go."

Then Elaine spoke up. "I'd like to help too."

Cole responded, "Elaine, I'd appreciate it if you with would stay here with Grace. I wouldn't want her to be alone in this storm."

Elaine persisted. "I know first aid."

"Elaine, I apologize, but I have to get going so I'll cut to the point. It's nasty out there. Tom is a big strong guy. You are not very big, and I'm pretty sure you're nowhere near as strong as Tom. You may be able to handle yourself – I don't know – but the thing is, I don't know that you do. And it would have to be your parent's decision and I don't have the time to wait. And to be honest, my answer would still be no. I'm sorry, but that's final."

Cole turned to go. "Tom, let's hit the road."

With an apologetic look to Elaine, Tom went to get his hard hat, heavy boots and foul weather gear.

Grace turned to Elaine. "Honey, would you mind helping me in kitchen?" A disgruntled young woman accompanied her.

Grace set about preparing a package of food and drink for her men. She worked quickly, knowing that Cole was out the door – gone – as soon as he had his kit assembled, with or without lunch and drinks. Elaine pitched in.

When Cole came in to say goodbye, Grace handed him the care package and took him aside.

"Grace, I gotta go."

"I know. If you hear that they need help with first aid or anything where we could be of help in a safe place, you get word to us. Now go. Love you."

"I love you." They kissed, and Cole turned and walked out.

When Grace turned back to Elaine, her eyes were glistening and fear showed on her face. As the guys headed for the door, Grace gathered herself and explained. "Elaine honey, I'm sorry you're unhappy, but I'm glad you're here, and for that matter, I'm glad I'm not out there. The simple fact is, Tom is a big strong boy – young man – and he's tough and smart. Would you like to sit and talk about it?"

Until mid afternoon the storm blew and rain assaulted the

house. It was the most violent weather Grace could remember – like a really bad thunderstorm, but it went on for hours. Twice power went out for an hour or so, but came back on before they had to worry about food in the freezer thawing. Elaine wanted to go out and have a look around, but Grace urged her not to until the wind died down. Finally around three it had slacked off significantly, so they went out together to check the house before it got dark and to have a look around the neighborhood. The wind still gusted, but the gusts were not the kind that had shaken the house earlier. Mostly it was very wet. Heavy rain still pelted down with brief periods where it slacked off before returning in soaking torrents.

Outside they found lots of branches down, but no obvious damage to the house. They steered clear of one tree at the edge of the woods that was leaning. They examined it carefully and decided that even if it did fall, it would miss the house. They crossed paths with one neighbor who was outside, but no one had a great deal to say. One end of their street was blocked off by a fallen tree. The other end was open, at least so far. Before long, their legs were soaked and rain was starting to find its way past their rain jackets, so they headed back to the house.

When they returned to the house, Grace broached the issue of where Elaine would spend that night. "It's a lot better out now, but I do not want to risk adding anyone to the list of people who need help. I think we should call your parents to see if they'll agree to have you spend the night here, if it comes to it. If we get word that it's safe, we'll get you to Izzy's house, but if not, I think it's better for you to stay." Elaine offered no objection.

They made a round of calls. Grace assured Elaine's mother that they had a guest room for Elaine and that conditions outside were not good – that the storm was worse than predicted, and it was safer to stay off the roads. After a little more discussion, Elaine's mother agreed that Elaine could spend the night with the Gradys if Grace thought it was best.

Several times that afternoon and evening Elaine found her thoughts drifting to Tom, and about how crazy it had been outside in the middle of the day – the violence of the wind and the intensity of the rain – and of being so close to him that night. She had to work to pull her thoughts away from something she was finding she wanted, but was not ready for. Not yet.

It was after midnight when the guys returned. Cole had checked in several times during the day – he knew that Grace worried. Still, she was relieved when the big-ass truck pulled into the driveway. When Cole and Tom walked in the door her heart surged with joy.

"Would you like some food? We can heat it up in a minute."

"I don't know if I'm more tired or more hungry. I guess the priority is some food and then sleep." He hugged Grace and they kissed.

He followed Grace into the kitchen and continued. "We'd a' been here an hour ago, but the neighborhood was blocked off by fallen trees. We went ahead and cleared a way for vehicles to get through. Thank god for the big-ass truck. It has enough grunt to haul some big hunks of wood. Less chainsawing and rigging lines for hauling that way. I'll check tomorrow to see if we can grab some of the downed branches and trees for firewood."

As his mom and dad talked, Tom and Elaine drifted into the living room. They hugged, and when their embrace loosened, Elaine saw tears in Tom's eyes.

"What's wrong Tom?"

"Uncle Joe – Dad's friend – got hurt. It's bad. He might die."

She was alarmed. "Oh Tom, I'm sorry. What happened?"

"It was really quick. There was a really strong gust, and a big branch came off a tree. It skewered him. I was standing right next to him."

"Oh my god! That's awful."

"All I could think about was it could have been you if you had come with us." Tom's eyes filled with tears.

"It could have been you, Tom."

They clung to each other.

A minute later a call came from the kitchen. "Food's on."

As the guys wolfed down some food, Grace explained that arrangements had been made for Elaine to spend the night. Tom and Elaine exchanged a quick glance, but quickly returned their attention elsewhere. As soon as they were done eating, the guys excused themselves, exhausted. As Tom headed to his bedroom, Elaine had to stop herself as she started to get up to follow. Instead she helped Grace clean up.

Although the day of the storm had been bad, it was the days

that followed that were the big story. As the Merrimack River rose, much of Plum Island disappeared beneath the flood waters. If not for the mandatory evacuation order for the island it would have been worse. As it was, five people died on the island. Their bodies were never found. Neither were the houses they were thought to have been in, the roads those houses had been beside, nor the land it had all sat on. Twenty more deaths were recorded around the region, mostly due to falling trees and other storm-related damage.

After the number of deaths, the most dramatic result of Gavin was the widening of the mouth of the Merrimack River. The jetties that had previously defined the mouth had been a thousand feet apart, separated by the main channel of the Merrimack. When the flood waters finally receded, there was no sign of either of them. The dunes in Salisbury were now separated from their Massachusetts cousins by a channel four thousand feet wide.

The entire tip of Plum Island was gone, including every single building in its Newburyport portion. A low sandy island was all that remained of the northern tip. It appeared that at some time during the storm the dunes opposite the Basin had breached and become a secondary channel of the river, cutting off the island's tip and with it, any hope of further evacuation. Tom could only imagine what went through the minds of people trying to get off the island when they faced a new channel as it attacked the new island from the south while the main channel swept it from the north and heavy wave action pounded it from the ocean side. Thinking about it made Tom shudder.

On the remaining part of Plum Island, most of the homes

within a mile of the original mouth of the river, were destroyed or seriously damaged. Along the remaining stretch down to the border of the wildlife refuge, the number averaged more like fifty percent. Damage on the Salisbury side of the river was not as bad, but still severe.

Newburyport's treasurer, a good woman, was shocked by the deaths and by the damage to Plum Island. But when she happened to think about the damage again, she was also shocked by the loss of real estate tax revenue that would soon hit the city. Her first reaction to the realization was to be appalled that she was thinking about tax revenues, given the suffering of so many people in the city, but still realized that she would have to make sure the mayor understood the implications for city finances as soon as she could.

Damage in Newburyport on the mainland was serious as well. Most of Water St. was underwater for days. Only small bits of Merrimack St. went under, but few homes between it and the river fared well.

Josef Fischer, Cole Grady's close friend, was in intensive care for two days after hours of surgery to save his life. Infection, caused by wood debris in his wounds, plagued his recovery. It was almost a month before he was released from the hospital. He was unable to return to the fire department for six more months, and when he did he was placed on light duty. By then it was clear that his recovery would never be complete.

The series of storms that hit Newburyport were unprecedented in the history of New England. No single one of the three storms was a record breaker, although the last storm – the one that ravaged Newburyport – came close.

Rough Road

For years people had been discussing how patterns of extreme weather seemed to be getting more and more locked in. Individual weather events were increasingly devastating as they grew more intense, but as with the Newburyport Nor'easters, sequences of merely serious weather events were emerging as a big problem. There was moderate flood damage across a wide swath of New England from the Newburyport Nor'easters, but nothing like what the Merrimack Valley had suffered. The similarity of the three storm tracks was raising alarms among planners who increasingly felt compelled to plan for how to prepare for and recover from significantly more intense local damage than ever before.

The tail end of Tom's cross country season was mostly washed out by the nor'easters. Between the weather and the upheaval it caused in Newburyport, Tom was not in top form for the state cross country championships. Even so, he was able to finish second in Division 2, closing in on a guy he had beaten by two seconds earlier in the season. Tom came very close to catching him. Everyone figured Tom was a shoo-in for a scholarship somewhere since earlier in the season his running had been as good or better than anyone in division one. However there was little fanfare in Newburyport – people were proud and happy about Tom's excellent finish, but other concerns dominated people's thoughts.

Part of the problem that Tom had struggled with as the cross country championship approached was sleep. Since the tornado he often found himself suddenly awake, having been dreaming of Elaine and the van as it shook and lurched. Since the Nor'easters it had become worse, with the van usually being replaced by his Uncle Joe being hurt. Sometimes Elaine, badly injured, was part of what he saw too. Afterward it would be awhile before he could get back to sleep. The night before the championship had been a bad one that way, with the result that he had been unfocused at the start of the race. Even though he understood why, Tom was frustrated that he hadn't done better.

School didn't reopen for three days after the floods subsided. When it did, the Climate Adaptation course once again had lots to talk about. One thing that changed in the class was a significant hardening of students' attitudes. Some climate deniers were still prominent on America's political stage. They now became the targets of great anger in the class. Mr. Rodriguez worked to tone down some of the more extreme sentiments expressed, but he found it difficult since he was even more angry and disgusted at a failing, flailing political establishment now that his own community had taken on momentary prominence in a terrible parade of weather and climate disasters around the world.

When the news review ended, Team Carbon struggled to stay focused on their project. As the course had progressed, Mace and Olivia had developed an increasingly powerful interest in political action at the expense of working on the project. Surging emotions colored the team's discussions that day. To a significant extent, the whole team now shared Mace and Olivia's sentiments. Certainly Elaine did.

That week Mace and Olivia got to work establishing a Newburyport High School chapter of the Climate Action Society. At the same time a chapter was started in the community at large. Engagement in the political movement around climate change became more intense both at the school and in the community generally.

Tom was interested in and supportive of the political activities of his friends. However, there was very little talk of it around home. His mother was not interested in political activism, although she had no problem with it in this case. Tom's father was a different matter. He had absolutely no use for politics generally and far less for political action. Needless to say, his aversion put a serious damper on discussion around the dinner table.

Chapter 11

Just before Christmas break, word got out that a bunch of new students were going to be starting in January. Coming on top of years of bad yields for a variety of reasons, this year's crop failures in the northern Midwest had been disastrous. In the hardest hit areas, nearly twenty percent of the farmers were going out of business, which created a domino effect with other businesses. Federal aid was in short supply, given a massive and rapidly growing federal debt and shrinking tax revenues. State aid around the Midwest was pretty much non-existent, with half the states in the region approaching bankruptcy.

Regenerative farmers, especially those with a decade or more of soil health improvements under their belts were better off than most, but a few of them were going out as well. The banks that held the loans for the failed farms made something from selling off the foreclosed farms' assets, but rarely did it cover the amount of the debts, given sharply depressed land and used equipment prices. Several of the most exposed banks failed. Much of the banking industry in the region now existed in terror of runs on their banks.

In Newburyport's schools, teachers were unhappy about the influx of students and how it would disrupt their classes, but everyone understood that there was nothing for it. Considering the empty seats from families displaced by Gavin, school administrators saw a bright side to the changes. Regardless, one way or another, everyone would have to cope.

After vacation, Team Carbon found out that one of the new students was signed up for the Climate Adaptation class. They soon learned that Mr. Rodriguez had assigned the new boy, Carter Johnson, to their team. In the first class he attended, Elaine welcomed him to the team. "Hi Carter, I'm Elaine Inoue. Welcome to Team Carbon. And to Newburyport."

"Thank you. Pleased to meet you."

"I'm Geoff Block. That's Geoff with a 'g'."

"Hi Geoff. Pleased to meet you."

"Izzy Giordano."

"Pleased to meet you Izzy."

"Hi Carter, I'm Olivia Hansen. Do people call you Carter or do you have a nickname?"

"Carter will do fine. Pleased to meet you."

"Tom Grady"

"Like the quarterback?"

"Uh, no – that's Brady with 'B'. I'm Grady with a 'G'."

"Oh, sorry about that." Carter offered an abashed grin. "Pleased to meet you, Tom."

"Mace Carter. We moved up here from Georgia last year."

"Pleased to meet you Mace. I guess I should be able to remember your last name." Carter smiled.

Carter's Midwestern accent and manners of speech intrigued the team. When they sat down and told Carter about their project, he became excited. "Is this the project they wrote up on the USCAS web site? Wait a minute – Mace, wasn't that you?"

"And Geoff. Yeah."

"That's pretty amazing."

Since Carter had been following the USCAS reports about their project, bringing him up to speed was pretty quick. When they were done, they asked Carter about his background.

Carter looked down and paused before responding. "I grew up on the family farm just outside Bismark. In North Dakota. My dad was an organic farmer. We had problems just like everyone else as the weather got worse. Dad was working on moving from regular organic farming to regenerative practices for a couple of years and doing pretty well at it. Then my mom got sick. She ran the business end of things. We didn't have good health insurance. Couldn't afford it. She died two years ago, right when the weather got so bad. Dad tried to hang on. My sister and I tried to help, but we couldn't do it. My mom's sister lives here and she's putting dad and me up until my dad can find work. My sister has a job in Bismark and stayed. That's mostly it."

There was a long moment of silence. Izzy was the first to find words. "Carter, I'm so sorry about your mom. I'm glad you're here."

Carter had tears in his eyes. "Thank you, uh, Izzy. That's kind of you."

There was an awkward pause. Elaine did her best to move on to happier issues. "So, you know, why don't we talk over the parcel of land by Mont Douamont again. I know we liked it when we talked about it before, but it might help Carter get up to speed and I don't think it would hurt to kinda run through it again."

The rest of the team agreed, happy to move beyond Carter's tragic story. They ran through the arguments for and against the parcel. The site they had chosen for the community core area was on the southern slopes of Mont Douamont, just south of the Gale River, and just over forty miles north of Amos. The plan was for the agricultural fields to surround it. People figured that a band of land along the Gale River would be a good wildlife corridor and preserved natural area, as would marshy areas elsewhere around the ring of agricultural lands they had in mind.

The peak of Mont Douaumont was the highest point for miles around. The lower peak at its base – the one they had climbed when they visited, looked more appealing as a location for the community core – was plenty high enough to be above any kind of flooding, but a location that probably got less wind than higher up on the hill. Plus the team was thinking it might make sense to reserve the peak as a site for a wind turbine. They described to Carter how a large part of the hilltop was exposed rock, which meant construction like that at New Thetford would be easy and they wouldn't use up arable land. Everyone still liked it, Carter included.

Over the course of the week they decided they liked the idea of a community of between ten and fifteen thousand people – a little less than Newburyport, but still not small. Izzy summed it up nicely. "If we make the population something like twelve or thirteen thousand people, it would be pretty much the same as Amos. It wouldn't be tiny or huge – just normal for people already living in the area. Lots of people living north of Amos could travel less to get to a town. Since some of the area is swampy, probably we should go for more than a half acre per person. Maybe like ten thousand acres for twelve thousand people. Plenty for wildlife and playing fields. A little park on Lac Kapejigwakogabawidj. Whatever."

They also came up with a name. Douamont was the first thought, but it translated to divine mountain, which nobody liked much. A bit of word play later somebody spouted 'Nousamont', which was an Americanized short version of something like 'we are going to the mountain' in French. The French was terrible, but the name stuck.

They decided to use free CAD and mapping tools to build a 3D model of the community, starting with an initial project to house maybe a hundred people, to help the team envision it. By the end of the week Geoff had created some great 3D graphics that showed what they were thinking about. The graphics were a huge hit with the class and were popular on the USCAS site when Mace and Geoff posted them.

The end of the following week saw the arrival of warm weather. Within days, every trace of snow was gone, and it kept getting warmer. In the middle of the following week early bulbs were poking up and buds on trees were getting fat. After lunch on Tuesday, Team Carbon got together outside for a little while after lunch to talk about Nousamont, and it was so warm that no one was wearing a jacket and people were rolling up their sleeves. When Tom looked at Elaine in the sun and with bare arms, it confirmed what he already knew. Although both Izzy and Olivia were good looking girls, they couldn't hold a candle to Elaine – not only the smartest person in the senior class, but also the most beautiful girl.

By the end of the week some new leaves were sprouting. Then the cold front blew in. Many farmers were distraught over the resulting damage to fruit trees and some other crops – yet another blow to their prosperity. People had enjoyed the warmth, but were left deeply uneasy over yet another climate anomaly.

In the first class after the cold front blew in, the Climate Adaptation class discussion was about how climate change was causing food prices to rise, and ways for people to adapt to yet another impact of extreme weather and unstable climate. Toward the end of the discussion Elaine shared her latest thinking about the impacts of climate change.

'You know, like, I'm thinking that the really big impact of

climate change isn't exactly the bad weather or big stuff like that. The really big thing – the worst part – is poverty. It's like Mace was explaining a couple of months ago. After the roof blows off your house three times in ten years or whatever, all of a sudden you aren't as prosperous as you were. If things were tough and money was tight before then, afterward it's really bad. People will have to make hard trade offs. Good food is expensive – maybe too expensive for some people. Maybe you can't pay the mortgage or maybe rent. I think that poverty is the real disaster caused by climate change."

When Elaine finished, the class was silent for a long moment.

Chapter 12

Elaine had started going to meetings of the Massachusetts chapter of the US Climate Action Society at the beginning of January, but in deference to his father's dislike of political action, Tom didn't start going with Elaine until after the bizarre January thaw. Even then, Tom's father was pretty unhappy with Tom's decision to start attending, but did nothing to stop him.

Tom's first meeting began with a welcome and general update. Then everyone divided up into breakout sessions for political action, mitigation action, or climate science. Elaine and Tom both attended the new break out session for mitigation action. The political action group was much better attended, but despite Elaine's interest in politics, she and Tom didn't care for its tone. They also figured that on the train ride home to Newburyport, Izzy, Geoff, and Olivia could fill them in since they were attending it.

During introductions Elaine mentioned their involvement with the Climate Change Adaptation class. A couple of people in the group made the connection to the Nousamont project, which people in the Mitigation Action group knew about.

"Are you two working on the Nousamont project?"

"Yes, we're members of Team Carbon. We're the ones doing the Nousamont project."

Another person commented, "Wow. You kids are doing great work. And – wait. Wasn't there something about a tornado when you were returning from a field trip up there?"

Elaine hesitated when responding, so Tom picked up the question. "Yeah. It was pretty crazy."

Other questions followed, but a few minutes later when there was no sign of them ending, the moderator nudged discussion back toward the agenda, to Elaine and Tom's relief.

Throughout the meeting Elaine and Tom received lots of encouragement and picked up some good ideas from others. They figured they should pass some great references and contacts for ultralight rail on to Olivia and Geoff. It was also obvious to Tom that Elaine's connection with the New Thetford project gave her a tremendous leg up on most people there. The attention she received as a result gave Tom a nice feeling. Elaine seemed a little uncomfortable, but the attention paid to this smart, beautiful girl – his girlfriend – made Tom feel good.

On the train ride home Olivia and Geoff were grateful for the rail info. It turned out the new info included some great car- and van-rail conversion projects they hadn't heard about yet. Even more exciting was news of a new company that was promising a complete 'from the ground up system', including new rail infrastructure, that was due sometime in the summer. Tom's interest in ultralight rail had been growing and he was intrigued by the conversion projects and curious about the new 'ground-up' initiative. More and more it was feeling like ultralight rail was the answer to the knotty transportation problems America faced. Its low-impact rail beds looked like a great replacement for the paved nightmares that highways had become. Together with super-efficient, car- and van-sized vehicles that could get incredible mileage and would be easy to run on electricity, ultralight rail was a bright spot in a future that was getting more and more scary.

However, most of the talk on the way home was about political action. Tom felt a lot of sympathy for it but little attraction. Very much like his father, Tom's passions were hands on problem solving and design. Elaine was clearly interested, but much more sensible than the other three, who talked a lot about shutting some things down and taking other things over. It was pretty clear that a schism was growing between traditional peaceful protest and more radical approaches in the political action group, and it was equally clear where Izzy's, Geoff's and Olivia's interests lay.

Chapter 13

Toward the end of February, news came out about sharp declines in purchases of consumer goods. The day after the report was issued, Mr. Rodriguez took up the topic in class. To get the discussion rolling, he made a proposition in the form of a formal debate – "Resolved: There is no relationship between climate change and the performance of an economy whose foundation is the manufacture and sale of consumer goods."

It didn't take long for the discussion to generate a consensus that the key problem in an economy with a strong focus on consumer goods was that it could lead to excess consumption, which would inevitably create more waste, and therefore greater climate impact. Olivia pointed out that, "as long as people equate lots of consumption with prosperity, it's going to be hard for them to not believe that greater consumption will lead to greater prosperity."

More discussion followed, which resulted in another consensus – that although there was undoubtedly a relationship between consumption and prosperity, there was no way it was a direct relationship. This was nicely summarized by Mace. "You know, I think prosperity is more about whether every person has decent shoes to wear than how many pairs you own. One thing is for sure – throwing out shoes just because you're tired of them has nothing to do with any kind of real prosperity. Certainly not if they're being produced instead of things that some people really do need." The class really liked how Mace made his point.

Chapter 14

As February ran its course, the relief over how normal the month had been was strong. With March's arrival, hope for spring grew stronger, even though New Englanders were all too well aware of how often weather in March could disappoint. However what followed, starting on March second, went far beyond what anyone could have imagined. A proper big snow storm struck. Over the course of the day, over eighteen inches of snow accumulated. Throughout the following week, the smallest accumulation of snow on any day was four inches. At the end of that eight day stretch, people were reeling from all the snow. They were grateful for the relief provided by the next three days, which were cold but clear.

However the forecast held little hope of real relief. Instead, it called for a storm that was significantly worse than the one that had started that winter's most severe stretch of weather. Thousands of people evacuated in anticipation, and those who remained stripped supermarkets bare and cleaned out hardware stores of every type of emergency supply. The local DPW and the state went into overdrive making preparations for what was predicted.

The next storm to hit was a Nor'easter. It dumped over two feet of snow and was followed by about six inches a day for the next four days. Main streets were kept open. People on side streets labored to maintain open pathways through the neighborhoods. By the time the next storm hit, things weren't good, but at least people were able to move around the community.

The next storm came in the form of a series of squall lines. By the time they had passed three days later another three feet had fallen. During the squalls, a large number of roofs collapsed. People struggled to keep access open to every house, with mixed success. A few days' break from snow helped, but even after the break, many people were still struggling desperately. A constant stream of evacuees left town, but getting clear of the mountains of snow was hard. As things continued to get worse, people found it best to travel north at least as far as Portsmouth, New Hampshire or even as far as Portland, Maine before heading inland to loop around the backside of the massive snow accumulations.

It was the following five days that were devastating. A foot of snow was followed by three, which was followed by another three, another two and finally another two feet. Eleven feet of snow in a five day period. Twenty three feet in just over two weeks. Generally the snow was light and fluffy, but all told its devastation far exceeded that of the terrible rainstorms in the fall. Hundreds of homes in Newburyport collapsed. Few of them were occupied, but by then there was no means of escape, no means of getting help to people. Scores died in collapsing houses. Scores more died from carbon monoxide poisoning when furnace flues were buried in snow. Hundreds more around the region died of more common weather-related causes.

The Inoue family left early – Mr. Inoue had taken a lesson from the terrible events of the previous six months. Elaine's pleas to stay behind fell on deaf ears. They were followed by the rest of Team Carbon except Tom and Carter – Tom because his father was determined to protect his home and needed Tom's help to do it, and Carter because he, his father, and his aunt had nowhere to go. Tom's family made it through in good shape. Carter's aunt died when a path bordered by snow walls over ten feet high collapsed on her.

Throughout it all, Tom worked harder than he ever had before, and his father worked harder than Tom. Digging out was a relentless task. Keeping the accumulation on their roof down was a chore that could not be deferred. It was essential to keep the structural load within reasonable bounds. Equally important was keeping the furnace flue open.

The hardest thing was finding places to put the snow. Snow cover varied between eight and fifteen feet for the most part, although many homes were entirely buried in drifts. When the snow stopped and as melting started, Tom and Cole spent countless hours cutting back the walls of shoveled walkways – far too many people had died when they collapsed. Cole had a close call when one collapsed and buried him. Only a quick reaction and a furious shoveling effort by Tom had saved his life.

As melting progressed, they were outside constantly, keeping the water draining. The heavy duty tractor with a front loader that Cole had moved to their house before the worst of the snowfall had set in was a godsend to the Gradys and their entire neighborhood.

All in all, the Grady family had it easy with three strong, healthy people to pitch in. Although they lost power, they had a generator which kept the furnace and refrigerator functioning, although under the circumstances the refrigerator was more a convenience than a necessity. Most of the heat for the house came from their wood stove. The Gradys did far more than their share in maintaining some semblance of access through the neighborhood and taking care of neighbors who were less fortunate. Neighbors tended to congregate at the Grady house during the day, and more than a few spent a cold night or two on their floor. A great many people were deeply grateful to the Grady family by the time it was over.

Given the amount of snow, the flooding that followed was minor, certainly in comparison to the fall flood. The walkways that had been carved for walkers became streams that worked reasonably well to carry snow melt to storm drains or, failing that, to the network of surface flows that found their way to the river. The biggest problem with them was constantly wet feet from water that could quickly grow deep when slush dams blocked drainage.

Damage around Newburyport was some of the most severe in the region, but the entire eastern coast of Massachusetts was a disaster, especially Boston's southern suburbs. Boston proper fared surprisingly well. Even so, their struggle was a tough one. The further west you went the less serious it became until at the New York State border it was merely a bad patch of winter weather.

Thanks to moderate, consistent melting of the snow, a few people were returning within two weeks after the last snowfall, although it was another week after that before the schools reopened. Many people never returned. The people who would never again leave the beleaguered communities around Boston were mourned.

The blizzards of March were a turning point in much of the northeast. People had had enough. People now understood what people elsewhere had been suffering for years. One result was a collapse in the real estate market. What had been pricey homes a year before now couldn't find buyers for half the price. This led to collapses in other parts of the economy. Thankfully the federal government had learned from the Great Recession and took up the slack when some lenders failed to provide loans to businesses that were holding their own, but that was about the limit of their support. Toxic politics and near gridlock in Washington had seemingly become a permanent feature in America's government.

When Elaine's family returned a couple of days before school restarted, Tom spent a lot of time at her place, helping them dig out. As Tom and Elaine worked together, they found themselves talking about their plans for the future.

"Tom, I can't believe how much snow this is!"

"Yeah, it's bad, but you should have seen some of the areas up our way. A few of them were a lot worse."

"No way!"

"Uh huh. A couple of those snow drifts were a good five feet more than the worst around here. The drifting around here isn't all that bad."

Elaine shook her head in disbelief and bent her back to shoveling. Ten minutes later she straightened up and leaned on her shovel. "I can't believe you aren't dead. You're doing twice as much as I am, and I'm losing it."

Tom leaned on his shovel and smiled. "But you're really decorative. And you're great company." Then he got serious. "I missed you, Elaine."

She walked over to Tom and wrapped her arms around him. "I missed you too." They held one another for a minute.

"Elaine, this is really great, but this snow isn't going to shovel itself."

"I guess, but this is more fun."

"Oh yeah. I guess I'll just have to make it up to you."

"I guess you will."

They got back to work. As they did, Elaine broached a topic that had been bothering her. "Tom, I've been thinking. I don't know if going to college is the right thing. I mean, Amherst seems like a great school. And the whole five colleges thing sounds great, especially since you're going to be at UMass. It's just that everything is so crazy."

"I know what you mean. I feel lucky I got in at UMass. I think maybe my cross country running made the difference. Anyway it sounds great, but with everything being so nuts, nothing really makes sense. And with everything going on, money is tight. I know what Mom and Dad would say – that we'll find a way – but I don't feel very good about it."

"Me neither. Dad makes good money and all, but Amherst is really expensive. And I've got sibs who will probably want to go college too. I just don't know."

What they didn't talk about was the recession that was rolling through the northeast. It was the worst anyone except the oldest people could remember – more similar to the Great Depression than the Great Recession. However, given the state of the economy and health care services, the number of old people was declining rapidly. What was far sadder was a high death rate among the very young due to a wide range of weather- and economy-related problems.

Thanks to a beautiful spring, the snow rapidly disappeared. However, the great weather did little to lift anyone's spirits. Even the beautiful weather itself was hard to fully appreciate, given how the impacts originating with January's thaw were now being felt by farmers and gardeners. But the real problem was that no one knew when the next shoe would drop. Everyone had become intensely aware that, these days, bad things tended to happen. Things were different now. There was no talk about rebuilding in flood plains any more, along with many other issues about how to handle climate-related problems. Disaster recovery and energy efficiency work were the only sectors of the construction industry that were doing well, which certainly helped the Grady family. Given the gratitude people felt to the Grady's, Cole rarely had to leave the neighborhood to get work. Unfortunately, competition for work was fierce, and gratitude only went so far when it came to choosing a contractor.

School routines were severely disrupted by the blizzards. Before schools reopened, empty chairs were removed from classrooms – no one wanted the reminders of the many friends who were now gone from their lives forever. Although the recovery from this trauma was slow for most people, things slowly moved toward something resembling normal. For Tom the experience during the snow emergency hadn't been as bad. The fact that his family had coped exceptionally well helped, and in some ways the more important thing was his family's success in rising to the extraordinary challenges and the recognition they received for their efforts.

The adversities the Climate Adaptation class students had suffered drew them together and motivated them. They buckled down like never before. Many of them helped out with night classes on climate adaptation that were instantly popular. Members of Team Carbon became minor celebrities around school.

The tail end of Tom's wrestling season was canceled and he decided to not do track in the spring, so Tom's high school athletics career ended with a whimper after his brilliant success in cross country in the fall and a very good wrestling season that saw some victories against top wrestlers around the region. Tom spent some of the time he saved by not doing track expanding his family's garden, although Elaine was the brains of that operation.

Chapter 15

Attitudes of people in Newburyport's two chapters in the Climate Action Society hardened further in response to the blizzards. The climate change vigil that had been consistent on Beacon Hill throughout the fall and winter was restarted before the cleanup from the blizzards was complete. It quickly became a large vigil – the focal point of protest in Massachusetts. It frequently appeared on national news outlets. Increasingly the vigil was split between people who simply wanted to make their presence known and a growing number of people demanding immediate, dramatic action. Newburyport was well represented every week.

As spring progressed, crowds grew ever larger, and on weekends were soon spilling over into the Common. By early May, the crowd was starting to spill over into the Public Garden at peak times. The state government had already been straining to cope with the impacts of extreme weather events, and now was spooked by demands for leadership and action by the vast crowd that now literally started on its doorstep, and sometimes spread across the next sixty acres.

The mood as the second weekend in May approached was unsettled. Through Izzy, Geoff, and Olivia, Elaine and Tom learned that direct action was afoot. Tom remembered echoes of previous discussions as they talked about 'storming the gates' of the State House and 'taking the State House grounds'. Those earlier exchanges may have been part of the reason why Elaine and Tom didn't take the talk seriously, to their later regret.

Saturday morning came and a large contingent of people from Newburyport, including most of the Climate Adaptation class, took the early train down to participate in the vigil. Things seemed pretty normal, although Tom did notice that Izzy,

Geoff, and Olivia all carried heavy backpacks. As they walked from North Station to Beacon Hill, they noticed an unusually large police presence, especially as they approached the front of the State House on Beacon St. When they arrived, Elaine and Tom headed over to talk to friends gathered near the gates. Tom noticed another, larger group of people gathered nearby, most of whom were wearing large backpacks. Then he saw the group split up into many smaller groups that headed for the gates and the surrounding fence. They started boosting each other up and over, into the State House grounds.

When he looked to the other side of the gate he saw Izzy, Geoff, and Olivia climbing up, and then saw Izzy wobble, thrown off balance by her heavy backpack, and fall to the bricked walkway below as she was preparing to climb over.

"Elaine, it's Izzy!" Together they ran over to help her as she lay on the ground. As they knelt down next to her they could see that she was conscious, but seemed disoriented. She had a bad bruise on her forehead.

At that moment a large contingent of police raced up and went after the people scaling the fences. As they went for Izzy, they muscled Tom and Elaine aside and started to lift the injured girl.

Tom's temper flared and he yelled angrily, "Hey, she's hurt! Leave her alone!" The next thing he knew he and Elaine were face down beside one another being handcuffed.

When Tom's parents arrived that afternoon to bail him out of jail his father was furious. When they got to the car he opened up on Tom. "What the hell were you thinking? God damn it, I didn't raise you to pull shit like that!" Tom tried to get a word in edgewise to explain as his father's tirade went on, but his father was having none of it. Tom's temper was building, and his mother could see it. She tried to calm her husband and gently put her hands on his free arm, which he was using to emphasize his harsh words. His father roughly shook them off.

"Hey! You be careful how you treat my mother. God damn it!"

It didn't go over well, to say the least. When his father stopped at the next intersection, Tom bailed out of the car and ran. His father's enraged voice followed, taunting him.

Badly shaken, Tom made his way back to the Common, staying well clear of any large groups of people. He wandered around feeling lost until he happened across Carter and some others from Newburyport. His relief was profound. They and the adults they were with listened as Tom explained everything that had happened. When Tom finished, one of the adults introduced himself.

"Hi Tom, I'm Cam Johnson – Carter's dad. I almost feel like I know you. Carter talks about you all the time – what a good guy you are. I want to let you know that this is all going to work out. It sounds like you really didn't do anything wrong, although yelling at a police officer when he's in action probably wasn't the best thing you could have done, even if he deserved it." Mr. Johnson wanted to call Tom's parents to let them know he was OK, but Tom wouldn't give him their number. He was still pretty shook up and was afraid of what his father would do.

In light of the impasse, Mr. Johnson took charge of organizing their prompt return to Newburyport on the next train. Back in Newburyport, Mr. Johnson gave Tom a ride home. When they got there, the Grady's car wasn't in the driveway. At Mr. Johnson's urgings, Tom now gave him his mother's phone number.

The call was brief and from what Tom could tell, it wasn't too bad. Mr. Johnson offered to Tom to wait with him until his parents returned. "Thanks Mr. Johnson, that would be really nice." He invited them in, where they sat in the living room and talked while they waited.

It was about a half hour later when they heard the car drive in. They all went outside to meet Tom's parents. The conversation between his parents and Mr. Johnson was brief and a bit tense, but calm and polite. Mr. Johnson and Carter said goodbye to Tom and were on their way. The Gradys made their way into the house in tense silence.

Once inside, Tom's father said, "I've never been so embarrassed in my life…" and seemed more than ready to start up again.

Tom's mom interjected with iron in her voice, "Cole, we talked about this on the way home. We are not going to have a fight like this in our home."

Cole stopped, then nodded and retreated to his shop in the cellar.

When the door to the cellar closed, his mother continued, "Tom, I do not want to ever hear you speak to your father in that tone of voice again."

"But he…"

"Tom, not ever again. I understand why your father was upset. That does not excuse some of the things he said. And no matter what he said, it does not excuse you. We are a family and we are going to act like it." She softened. "Honey, do you understand what I'm saying?"

Her softer tone broke his anger. Tom slumped. "Yeah Mom. I'm sorry."

She hugged him. "That's more like it. Let's go get something to eat. I'm hungry and I bet you're starved. Then I want to hear the story – all of it."

Together they made three sandwiches, two of which were enormous. Tom poured three glasses of milk. When things were ready, Grace grabbed one enormous sandwich and a glass of milk and headed downstairs. "I'll be back in a flash."

A few minutes later she came back up. "Now where were we?"

After Tom had laid it all out for her, his mother summarized, "So you were nearby, minding your own business when Izzy took a bad fall while she was doing something she shouldn't have done. You and Elaine went to help her. When a police officer started to move Izzy roughly, you yelled at him that she was hurt – none too politely by the sound of it. Is that about it?" Tom agreed. "Maybe you should have been more polite. Regardless of who was right or wrong, it might have worked better."

Although it pained him to agree, he did and added. "That's pretty much what Mr. Johnson said."

"I think I could get to like this Mr. Johnson. OK, we'll get this sorted out. Your dad is mostly calmed down. I know you didn't mean to upset him and you really didn't do anything – well not much of anything – wrong. You need to give him some time to sort through things. It's just the way he is, and he has lots of things he's worried about. He holds it in, but it eats at him. I think that's most of what you were seeing today.

"Just so you know, none of this means he doesn't love you. I don't know if a young man like you can understand how much a father loves his children. That hasn't changed a bit – he loves you and would do anything for you. With that said, a little less yelling would be good. Would you like some pie?"

Tom offered no objection, so his mother took half a cherry pie out of the refrigerator, cut two large slices and stuck them in the microwave. While waiting for the microwave she stuck a couple of dishes in the dishwasher. A minute later she returned to the microwave and pulled the pie out, set a slice and a fork in front of Tom, and headed downstairs with the other slice. Looking over her shoulder she advised, "Careful, it's hot. Back in a sec."

Tom waited. He felt like he should be thinking things through, but mostly he just sat, a bit numb from the day's events. He was grateful to his mother for bringing sanity to the mess. It also occurred to Tom that hot cherry pie smelled pretty darn good. That was about as much thinking as Tom managed for the maybe two minutes before his mother returned and asked, "More milk?"

"Maybe a half glass. Thanks."

There was little conversation while he finished eating. When he was done he said, "Thanks Mom."

She took his big hand in her two smaller ones. "It's going to be OK. We'll talk to our lawyer on Monday and get the wheels turning. We'll work it out."

"I know. Uh, Mom. I'd like to check in with Elaine to make sure she's OK."

"OK honey. Love you."

"I love you Mom."

In his room Tom pulled out his phone and keyed Elaine's number.

Elaine picked up. "Are you OK?"

"Yeah, I'm fine. How about you?"

"I'm fine. Once we got to the station, the police were OK. My mom and dad were pretty freaked out. They were really worried that I was hurt or freaking out or something, but it was OK. I mean totally weird, but OK. What happened with you?"

"It wasn't too bad until I got into the car with Mom and Dad. Dad kinda went crazy. I've never seen him mad like that. He said some bad stuff. Mom tried to calm him down but he was pretty crazy. I kinda yelled at him and when I saw the look on his face I jumped out of the car and ran."

"Oh. Wow. That's bad."

"Yeah. I kinda walked around and found Carter and some people. Carter and his dad brought me home and hung around

while we waited for my parents to get here. After they left –
after Mom and Dad got home – things with Dad looked like
they were maybe going south again, but my mom put her foot
down. I guess things're better now. I hope."

"Tom I'm so sorry. You didn't even do anything wrong."

"Well Mom and Mr. Johnson both said maybe it wasn't too
smart to yell at that cop the way I did."

"OK, I see that. Oh wait! The whole thing was on the news!
Two stations, maybe more. Like the whole thing. You looked
really good and the policeman who was being rough with Izzy
looked really bad."

"Is Izzy OK?"

"Yeah, I guess. They took her to the hospital, but they say it's
only for observation. She'll probably be out tomorrow."

"That's good. I was a little worried. Huh, so I was on the
Boston news. I bet Dad won't like that."

"No, no – you were on national news. I guess the Boston vigil
is a pretty big deal. Lots of places are copying it, and this is the
first time there was any kind of violence or anything. I mean I
guess no one was exactly violent, but there were like a hundred
people arrested."

"Uh, no. National TV. That's bad. I don't think Dad's going to
like that at all."

"Tom, you were a hero, kinda. Standing up for a girl in
distress. You know."

"I dunno. It doesn't sound so bad the way you say it."

"Because it wasn't bad. You were pretty darn good. Maybe not perfect, but nobody is. Tom, you are a great guy and I'm really lucky you like me."

"Elaine, I'm the lucky one. I wish we could be together all the time."

They talked for a long time, eventually coming around to the topic of going off to college. Neither one wound up feeling like it was the right thing to do.

When they hung up, Tom read for a while and was about to call it a night when there were footsteps outside his door and a knock. "Can I come in?" It was his father.

"Yeah. OK Dad. Come in." Tom tensed up, not knowing what to expect.

His dad came inside and was quiet for a second. Not knowing what to think, Tom started to explain. "Dad, I'm sorry about yelling at you, and for getting arrested and everything. I…"

His father cut Tom off with a wave of his hand. "Tom, I'm not angry. What I am is a dumbass. I'm the one who should be sorry. I'm really sorry I blew up at you."

The knot that had been tying Tom up inside evaporated. He choked out, "No Dad, it's not like that. I should have been smarter about it. I shouldn't have let it happen. I guess it got on TV and the web. I'm really sorry."

"Nope, don't be sorry. Don't worry. You did pretty good. Pretty darn good. You know how I know that?" Tom shook his head, "I know 'cause I watched the news clips. All of them. You probably shouldn't have yelled at that cop, but you were helping your dumbass friend who went and got herself hurt. By the way, she's going to be OK. Her folks called to let us know and to thank you for helping her. They were really grateful for what you did. They said lots of nice things about you and Elaine. Anyway, I am proud of you. And I can't tell you how sorry I am for the way I acted. Can you forgive me?" Tears welled up in Cole's eyes.

"Yeah Dad. Sure. Of course."

Cole came over and wrapped his arms around Tom. "I'm sorry."

"Dad I shouldn't have yelled at you. I'm sorry too."

Cole sat back up. "Well I guess it's late. Tom, I love you, and I'm proud of you."

"'Love you too Dad. You're a great dad."

Before he could choke up again, Cole murmured, "Sleep tight."

Chapter 16

Sunday was very uncomfortable for Tom. The news media were camped out in front of the house and pounced on passers by for any kind of background information about Tom while they waited. At one point, Mrs. Henniker who lived two doors down, was swarmed by reporters when she walked by. With the windows open he could overhear her as she took them to task. "Tom is a very nice young man. The Grady's are a wonderful family – always helping other people out. You should all be ashamed of yourselves. You're acting like a bunch of vultures. You should go away and leave them alone." Although the reporters didn't leave, Mrs. Henniker's words made Tom feel better.

His mother went out once for some errands and reporters swarmed her car as she backed out. The police officer who had been sent to keep an eye on things had to help her get out of the driveway and on her way. After his mother returned and the press showed no sign of moving on, Tom snuck out the back way from the house to avoid them, and headed into town. He found some friends before long, but Saturday's events were pretty much the only thing they wanted to talk about. However they were the last thing Tom wanted to deal with. Before long he headed over to Elaine's house, but when he saw the reporters there, he headed home instead.

Showing up at school on Monday was a nightmare. A few reporters noticed him on his way to school and set out in pursuit. Tom put his running abilities and intimate knowledge of the city to work and quickly lost them.

In school, he couldn't walk down a hallway without drawing a crowd. Mostly Tom was able to ignore it, but when a couple of guys he didn't get along with really got on his case, it came close to turning into a fight. Quick action by a couple of Tom's friends, including 'Tiny' Boynton – the star offensive tackle for the football team – defused things. Tom thanked his friends for stepping in, but wound up realizing he was just going to have to suck it up and be able to take some shit from assholes.

Grace was in touch with their lawyer first thing. As soon as they hung up, the lawyer got right to work. She wanted to make certain that what should be a simple matter didn't turn into something more. Media attention and political agendas could easily poison the legal process, to her client's detriment. Since any actual offenses were minor at worst – at least in the larger scheme of things – steering the situation past these hazards was her priority.

By the end of the day she had arranged a meeting with representatives from the police department and the prosecutor's office to see whether it might just all go away. At the very least, she wanted to know what her client faced now that everyone had had a chance to calm down.

By the end of the week, things had mostly returned to normal. The national coverage of the incident on Beacon Hill had gone international. Tom had continued to refuse interviews, and on Tuesday his lawyer had given a mild statement that made the Boston Police look good. She talked about how her client's outburst, though well intended, had done nothing to help the situation, and how her client respected the Boston Police and the hard work they did. This was followed by a Thursday meeting that resulted in an agreement to drop all charges against Tom and Elaine. The arresting officer was there, and after things broke up, he approached Tom and Elaine.

Their lawyers watched like hawks as he offered his hand to Tom,"No hard feelings?" His manner was gruff, but the tone was conciliatory.

"Naw. Sorry for yelling at you."

"No problem." He turned to Elaine and offered her his hand.

"Miss Inoue?"

"Yes."

"Are we OK?"

"Yes sir. It was all kind of crazy and it all ended up OK. I'm OK. Thanks."

The cop gave her a skeptical smile when she thanked him.

"You know. For coming over and being nice."

"In that case, you're welcome. You kids have a good day. Stop by and say 'hi' if you see me at the vigil. Keep up the good work." He turned to Tom. "You're a lucky guy. She's a good one."

"Well, you know what they say – better lucky than smart."

The cop just smiled and gave a wave as he went on his way.

Chapter 17

Although he was happy with how the whole affair with the police concluded, Cole Grady was still stressed by everything going on. Over the previous year, the economy had gone from bad to worse. A couple of other contractors in the area had gone out of business despite all the work in repairing weather damage. And despite his many loyal customers, Cole was hanging on by his fingernails. In the fall he'd had to let two long-time employees go for a time during the middle of the winter with the expectation, or at least the hope, that he would be able to rehire them in the spring. Tom knew them both well and knew they were good carpenters and good guys. He could see what it was doing to his father.

School finished up well for Tom. Team Carbon's project was very well received, and he got his first A+ ever in a course. His other courses were good too. His parents were very proud. As always, Elaine's grades were top.

Commencement was subdued. Elaine gave the Valedictorian address. It was all about how everyone was responsible for making the world a better place, and it was very warmly received. Several speakers said nice things about the work by Team Carbon. For Tom that praise and Elaine's speech were the high points of the big event. Despite the terrible events of the year that culminated in this day, it gave Tom hope for his classmates and himself. However even on a really good day like commencement, that hope was tempered by the fear of what the coming year would bring.

Elaine's parents were hosting a graduation party, so Tom's choice of which one to attend was easy. His mom and dad dropped Tom off, and stayed around for a while to talk with the Inoues. Tom and Elaine disappeared to congratulate each other in their own way. A couple of minutes later they returned and joined the party.

Twenty minutes later, Tom's parents came to tell him they were leaving and to call if he needed a ride. A minute or so after that, Elaine's parents came out and sat down with Tom and Elaine.

"Elaine, honey, your Dad and I have a surprise for you – a

graduation present. We're getting a new second car and have decided to give our old one to you. Now we'll understand if you don't want to keep it. It's fine with us if you sell it, but we are so proud of you and we wanted to let you know just how proud and happy you have made us."

As her mother had surmised, Elaine was of two minds. "Wow. Thanks Mom. Thanks Dad. That's great!" It was mostly Elaine's mother who was able to pick up on the internal conflict that lay behind her daughter's words.

"OK honey. This is your day, so have fun." She kissed Elaine's forehead, and reached over and gave Tom a kiss on the cheek. "You too Tom."

Elaine's dad gave her a big hug and shook Tom's hand.

When they were alone, Tom opened up. "Wow, a car. That's great. But it's pretty weird too."

"Yeah I know. I don't really know how to feel about it."

"I guess you should take your time deciding – no rush."

"Yeah, good point. Maybe we could go somewhere."

"Yeah, sure." Then they went and joined the rest of the party.

There was a lot of dancing and talking. Mrs. Inoue gently separated a few couples making out in corners. Although the party was intended to be alcohol-free, an hour or so after it started a couple of friends came in who'd had a head start in that department. Mr. and Mrs. Inouye welcomed them to the party, and then Mr. Inoye took the driver of the car aside and informed her that they would be happy to give the kids a ride anywhere they wanted to go, and pointedly suggested that he would be happy to hold onto her car keys. With Mr. Inoue's eyes boring into her, the driver reluctantly relinquished her keys. Tom observed the interaction from a distance, all too aware of how intense Mr. Inoue's stare could be.

Over the course of the party, an idea emerged. "Elaine, you know what we should do?"

"Tom Grady, you have a one track mind!" she teased.

"Uh. Uh. Let me start again. I have an idea of what we should do in your car."

Elaine was relentless. "Tom Grady, you are incorrigible!!"

"Ahgh! I give up. Let's take a road trip to New Thetford. I'd really like to see it."

"Oh, why didn't you say so?" Her mischievous smile looked up at Tom as she snuggled up next to him.

"You know girlfriend, you can be tough on a sensitive guy."

"OK, but what does that have to do with a tough guy like you. Anyway, you always tell me how soft I am."

"Soft but tough. And me, tough but sensitive. What a pair."

Elaine smiled. "We make a good pair."

"And speaking of really good pairs!" Tom grabbed Elaine's waist, eliciting a squeal. His hands were moving north when she leaned in and kissed him. As intended, Tom was distracted from his exciting but too-public exploration of her body.

A minute later they had calmed down. "Tom, I like your idea

for a road trip. You should see New Thetford. And I want to visit my Aunt Jill and catch up on what's going on there."

As they talked, Carter drifted by and, overhearing the topic, he paused. "You're going up to New Thetford?!" The three of them talked for few minutes before the topic shifted and Carter moved on.

Tom was the last to leave the party that evening, lingering to spend more time with Elaine. Things had been so crazy and they still were, but now that they were done with high school, things were different. Together they talked more about their second thoughts about college. The world was a little crazy. Maybe more than a little. They both knew that having a college degree would be a great thing, but Tom had the feeling that by the time he could be finished, it might be a lot less valuable than things he might do instead. They talked about it and enjoyed their intimacy as they talked. Elaine was thinking the same way – that the choice they had to make was quite different than it would have been in more normal times. As they kissed and held one another, conversation waned and their passion grew. Elaine put the brakes on. "Tom, I want you. I want to make love to you. More than I know how to say. I'm just not sure that this is the right time. That I'm ready."

Tom's mind was spinning. "Oh god, I want you so bad. But it has to be right. I love you Elaine. But if we aren't going to make love, I have to leave. I'm about to go crazy I want you so bad."

They lay beside one another for a minute, silent. Tom got up, leaned over and kissed her on the cheek. "See you tomorrow?"

"I sure hope so." Her smile was both worried and hopeful.

The next morning as Tom was still lazing in bed, he reached over, grabbed his phone, and hit his favorite number. Elaine picked it up on the first ring. "Hi."

"You're probably up and at 'em. What did you have for breakfast?"

"Well, when I get up, IF I get up, I'll have to figure that out, won't I? What about you?"

"I'm still in bed."

"Why don't you get out of bed and come over here."

"Will you still be in bed?"

"You have a one track mind."

"Pretty much. But you can't blame me since the most beautiful, smartest, sexist woman in the world is in your bed at the moment."

"Ahhh. I knew there was a reason why I love you."

"There are lots of reasons why I love you."

"Why don't you come over and we can talk about it? What would you like for breakfast?"

"Isn't it obvious?"

"Let me rephrase – I'm going to be in the kitchen making my breakfast. Can I make something for you?"

"Hmm. I guess I'm out of witty responses. How about whatever you're having, times two."

"See you soon."

"Bye."

Tom hopped out of bed and quickly dressed. His mom and dad were at work so he left a note.

When he got to Elaine's, she was at the door waiting. Once he was inside and the door was closed they embraced and shared a long passionate kiss. When it had run its course Elaine leaned back. "Let's go up to New Thetford."

"Yeah, I like that idea a lot."

"I need to talk to my mom and dad and check with my aunt. Let's go tomorrow."

"Sounds great."

"OK, let's eat."

By mid morning they were all set. Both sets of parents hesitated a bit, but didn't take long to come around. Elaine's aunt was all for it.

They spent the rest of the day making preparations. Elaine tried out her new car a little and then started it charging. She figured they should probably make it there on a good charge – her new/older car didn't have the range of newer cars like her dad's replacement van and her mother's new car. Just in case, they also checked out quick charging station locations along the way. By noon they were packed and ready. After lunch they headed downtown to see who they could find.

When they hit the bullnose, a favorite downtown meeting spot, they found a group of friends hanging out. They talked for awhile, and then mentioned the trip they were planning. Everyone was interested, especially Carter.

"You're lucky to know someone who lives there, Elaine. It's exciting, what they're doing."

She glanced at Tom. Their ESP was working. He nodded. "Carter, why don't you come along? Tom and I would love to have your company."

"What? Really?"

"I'd have to talk to my aunt, but I bet she'd be OK with it."

"Wow, that would be amazing if I could come. You're sure it would be OK?" Elaine assured him that it would. "Tom, you're OK too? I mean…"

"Carter, its fine. Really."

"Wow, I gotta call my dad, just to make sure."

It was a short conversation. "Dad loves the idea. I'm in."

"OK then. Let me check with my aunt." Elaine got her and explained what a good guy Carter was and how excited he was, and how much he knew about farming. When Elaine finished and hung up she reported. "She's good with it, but we'll need a tent."

"I've got one. And camping stuff."

"That's great, Carter. Tell you what – go get your stuff together and let's get everything packed up so we'll be ready to head out. Meet at my house in like an hour?"

"This is great. See you in an hour." Carter set out for home at high speed, feet flying.

Tom laughed, "Man, is he excited or what."

"You're OK with him coming?"

"Yeah. I like Carter. It'll be fun."

They headed back to Elaine's house, taking their time. Her house was to the southeast of downtown, a little further out and nearer to the water than Carter's. They stayed along the river for as long as they could, down past the fishing pier and along the rail trail, taking their time. Shortly after they got to Elaine's house, Carter showed up. They stowed his stuff in her car. When everything was set, they headed into her house to hang out.

"Thank you guys for letting me come with you. I've really wanted to see New Thetford. I'm really pumped."

"Jeez Carter, I guess you are. It's not a big deal – plenty of room. No sweat, man."

They talked for a bit when Tom had an idea. "You know, maybe we could leave today. Maybe tonight. Then we could have all day tomorrow there. And we're not really doing anything tonight."

"Huh. I like it. I could call my aunt to see if it was OK, but she's pretty cool. Carter, what about you?"

"Sure. Whatever you want is good with me. I'd have to check with my dad, but I can't imagine he'd have any problem."

"OK then."

"Wait a sec. I just had another idea. Maybe I could talk my mom into having you guys over for dinner tonight."

"That sounds really good Tom, but I think my dad might want me to spend a little time with him before we go. I wouldn't want to leave him alone, especially since we'll be gone for a few days."

"Maybe he'd like to come for dinner too."

"I dunno. Seems like probably. I think he'd probably like it."

"Elaine, what about your folks?"

"I would guess so, but you should probably call your mom before we, like, make any plans."

"You got it."

It was another quick call.

"She's good. Everyone's welcome, the more the merrier. We just have to give her a head count."

The other two got on their phones. Carter was the first one to finish. "It'll be Dad and me. Dad'll bring brownies and stuff from work for dessert."

Elaine was finishing her call as Carter reported. "We're good too. Mom, Dad, Jody, and Mike. That makes seven plus you guys. Mom and I'll do a big salad."

"OK, ten it is."

"Hey guys, I should get home and take care of a few things before dinner. What time should Dad and I be there?"

"Mom said six." It wasn't a minute before Carter was out the door and on his way home.

"Tom, this is going to be fun. Dinner was a great idea."

"Well, you're providing the wheels and a place to crash. It seemed like the least I could do. Speaking of wheels, I should beat feet so I can help get ready."

After making their goodbye's, Tom headed home.

A few minutes after six, Carter and his dad showed up at the Grady house and were ushered in. Tom's mom accepted the Terrill Malden, Inc, chocolate treasures gratefully. "Cam, you shouldn't have, although I know one young man who will help eat this up – brownies are his favorite. An older man too, although he probably shouldn't."

"Well since I'm working there it was easy. But it is a nice perk. Thank you for having us over."

"I have been wanting to really meet you so I could thank you for the help you gave Tom – the day at Beacon Hill and the mess with Izzy and the police. It was a hard day for us, and you made it much better. I can't tell you how grateful I am."

"You're welcome Grace. When I tell you it was my pleasure, it truly was. Tom and Elaine have both helped Carter feel welcome here. I'm sure you can understand how grateful I am for that. My heart ached for Tom and went out to you and Cole as he told us what happened. He is a fine young man, and providing help to him was no burden. It was one more of the joys in my life. I thank the Lord I was able to help."

Grace, touched by Cam's sincerity and Midwestern grace, was

trying to construct a reply when the van that had replaced the one totaled by a tornado pulled up, and a small army piled out. While Elaine's mom hauled out just about the largest bowl of salad Tom had ever seen, Grace smiled at Cam and briefly grasped the back of his hand, and headed off to welcome the new arrivals. She directed Elaine, the other two road trippers, and Elaine's two sibs, to the back yard with the instruction that the road trippers should entertain the kids while the adults went inside.

Dinner was a success, with shocking numbers of hamburgers and brownies disappearing in the process – a testament to the metabolism of teenagers, especially eighteen year old boys. As people sat around talking, most of the topics were happy ones as befitted the happy occasion. However as dessert was wrapping up, Cam Johnson broached a topic of a different sort.

"So Cole. And I guess Grace, Manda, and Hiro too. What have you heard about the rise of lawlessness recently? Some of the people at work seem pretty worried about how law and order isn't what it once was. Of course the news people are all over that kind of thing, but you never quite know what to make of their reports, especially about colorful news like this. I do hear from some of my old friends in North Dakota of some bad things going on out that way."

Hiro was the first to respond. "I hear the same kinds of things around here. Not Newburyport so much, or any of the towns around here, but in poor areas in Boston and other cities, and in remote areas north of here, I guess things aren't always that good. Certainly worse that even just a year ago."

Cole added,"I hear the same kind of thing. Mostly things are

OK in most places, but with cuts in police budgets everywhere, like you and Hiro say, things aren't as good as they used to be."

The discussion about the rise in lawlessness went on for a few minutes before the topics of discussion moved back to happier ones.

A little later on, Cole tipped his head toward Tom. "Could you give me a hand with something?"

"Sure thing, Dad."

They headed in the direction of the grill, but before they got there Cole Grady paused. "Tom, I'm glad you're doing this trip. It's a great idea. Just one thing. I mean besides the regular dad stuff about being careful and all that – which you'll get plenty of from your mom anyway."

"So Dad, what's up?"

"Well, like we were talking about earlier, the word from up that way – like in the middle of nowhere in New Hampshire – is that there's been more crime than there used to be. Some bad stuff. I kind of downplayed it a little to not worry your mom or the others too much, but it worries me. I thought about it just now and, especially since you're going to be going at night, we might want to do something about it."

"OK."

"What I want is for you to have something with you that will give you an edge, if it comes down to that. Maybe your folding hunter knife – the one that locks. I assume you still have that? Is it sharp?"

"Yeah, it's pretty good." Tom took a knife from his pocket.

"Can I take a look?"

Tom handed it to his father, who quickly assessed it. "It's pretty good. It's a well-made knife – good and strong, but it could be sharper. How about if I touch it up for you?"

"Sure thing, Dad."

"And I know we've talked about this before, but the world is a little different now. What is your most important weapon?"

"My head – my mind."

"Good. Keep your head when the shit hits the fan and you're a big step ahead. Step one in taking control of a bad situation is a plan. What's next?"

"Run away if you can. If you can't, speed and aggression."

"Good. There's lots more, but I don't think you're going to need any of it. I want you to have the time of your life. I'll be back up with the hunter in five minutes or so. Oh, could you go check on the grill – make sure it's not going to burn the house down or anything?" Cole headed downstairs to his shop, while Tom headed out back to check the grill.

Good to his word, Cole was back a few minutes later and slid Tom his knife, which Tom tucked back into his pocket.

It was almost dark before things started to wind down. Before the three new grads headed out, the requisite pictures were taken, hugs shared, and kisses bestowed. Then they piled into Elaine's car and hit the road.

Chapter 18

It was a beautiful night and excitement was high. High school was history and the future opened in front of them, which on the one hand was frightening, and on the other carried hope and offered fulfillment of a thousand dreams. That, plus they were literally on the road to one of the best places in the world, as they saw it.

The miles rolled by and they talked about a million things. As they peeled off Route 93 onto 89 just south of Concord, NH, Tom started to feel the need for a pit stop to relieve the pressure from the extra hamburger and several brownies he had eaten. But he figured it was like maybe an hour until they were in Thetford, and he didn't want to break the spell of the amazing evening. However as they went along, the pressure increased relentlessly until finally he had to speak up. "Hey guys, is anyone else interested in a pit stop?"

The others allowed as how they wouldn't mind it, so Tom, again acting as navigator, found a rest stop in Grantham, NH that looked promising.

Elaine approved. "Yeah, I've stopped there before when we went to visit my aunt. It seemed like a nice place."

By the time they were peeling off the highway for the rest area exit, Tom's need to relieve himself was becoming urgent. However when they got to the rest stop building, all the inside lights were off and the door was locked. There was a sign listing reduced hours of operation due to budget cuts.

"Guys, sorry, but I'm heading for the portapotties over there."

As he hustled toward a cluster of plastic outhouses near some bushes, he heard Elaine's car as she relocated it to a closer point and parked.

Several minutes later, after the others had used other units and returned to the car, Tom was finishing up. As he did, he saw lights that looked like maybe someone coming off the highway. By the sound of it, they parked next to Elaine's car. Two – maybe three – people got out.

He was about ready to go back to the car when he heard a scuffle and the sound of a fight, and Carter yelling. Then Elaine screamed.

When Elaine screamed, Tom almost rushed out to fight the attackers when his father's words came back to him – to use his head and take control of the situation. Tom clamped down on his emotional response and instead quickly assessed the situation. He took out his knife, opened it and checked that the blade was locked before he slipped out of the portapotty and ducked behind it. Two men had grabbed Carter and were dragging him toward some bushes not far from where Tom was. They were taking turns beating him as he resisted. A third man was dragging Elaine toward a different section of bushes. She was struggling noisily, but the guy was strong and paid no attention except to viciously twist her arm when she tried to kick him.

As Tom slipped behind the row of bushes and moved quietly to where Carter and his assailants were heading, his urge to go to Elaine's aid was powerful. He had to force himself to stick to his plan. Tom double checked that his knife's blade was locked open. The two men beating Carter had paused, breathing hard from their violent workout. They stood with their backs to Tom, maybe ten feet away. Tom crept up behind them. One of them was starting to turn when Tom jammed his knife into the man's ass cheek. The guy screamed and then screamed again as Tom wrenched and twisted his knife out. As he was going down, Tom shoved him into the other guy. As the other guy was fumbling with his friend, Tom tackled him and rammed the knife hard into the man's thigh. He screamed louder than the first one and again when Tom worked his knife free.

Tom sprang to his feet and turned toward the third man. Tom's emotions flared as he saw Elaine running toward him. However her assailant was chasing her, so Tom tweaked his plan and headed to intercept him.

"Elaine, take care of Carter. If the others try to get up, kick 'em where it hurts. Hard as you can." Then he turned his full attention to the third man. They faced off, Tom with his knife, and the other man with a tire iron in his hand.

"Leave now and you live, asshole." Tom was furious – angrier than he had ever been – but was cold. His focus on ending the threat they faced was absolute.

"Motherfucker!" The man lunged at Tom and started to swing the tire iron at Tom's head. Tom was ready and lunged forward to get inside the tire iron's arc. Mostly it worked. Tom was able to partially block the blow and the tire iron glanced off his shoulder. It hurt like hell, but through the pain Tom used his knife to viciously slash the attacker's ribs.

The attacker screamed and staggered back. He pawed his ribs with his free hand and it came back bloody. "I'm gunna beat your head to a fucking pulp and then fuck that girl and kill her too."

"Last chance. Leave."

The instant Tom saw the other guy start to move, Tom drove into him low, hard, and fast. Still driving forward, Tom plunged his knife into the attacker's torso. The tire iron struck low on Tom's back, but with an awkward angle, there little energy behind it. Tom ignored it and stabbed again, and then again. The other guy got in another swing with even less energy behind it as Tom drove his knife into the guy's ribs, hard. The guy went rigid for a moment and then slid to the ground. Tom stepped back and watched as a pool of blood started to grow. The man's eyes closed.

As Tom watched life depart his enemy's body, his mind tried to make sense of what had just happened. Instead, Tom's emotions deflated – collapsed. The emptiness that now filled that place left Tom with clarity and a mission, and a new, profoundly alien perspective of himself in the world. Tom bent down to retrieve his knife from between the man's ribs. He did more damage as he had to twist and pry it before he could get it free. The man just lay there, inert – empty.

Tom went back to help Carter and Elaine. The other two men had flopped further away from Carter and Elaine. When they saw Tom approaching, his knife in his hand and dripping in their friend's blood, and then saw the look on his face, they wriggled further back. Terror plastered their faces.

Carter was badly battered. Elaine had him sitting up and he seemed to be awake and aware. Elaine was favoring one wrist – the one she had been dragged by.

Tom aimed a vicious glare at Carter's two assailants and they fluttered their hands in submission. He knelt down beside his friends. "Elaine, are you OK?"

"My wrist hurts but it's not too bad. I think my knee is skinned pretty badly. Mostly I'm OK."

"Carter?"

"Hurts. Lots of places." He groaned.

"OK. Anything in particular? Move around a little bit. Easy. Just to see if you can."

Carter did, obviously with lots of discomfort. "I think the worst is my hand, where I hit one of 'em."

"Huh. I guess that's good. Well not good, but you know what I mean. Do you want to get up? We should get you to a doctor."

"I guess. Can you give me a hand?"

"Sure. Just a sec." As Tom folded his knife and slid it into his pocket he directed a vicious glare at Carter's assailants. They cringed back.

Tom slid his forearm under his friend's left arm from behind. Elaine did the same under his right arm.

"Does that feel OK?"

"I guess."

"OK, try to get your feet under you. Slow and easy. Easy now. Lift."

Tom did most of the initial lifting but as they got Carter up a little, he took over.

"You doing OK?"

"It isn't too bad." Carter exhaled heavily as pain ran through his body.

"Tell you what, let Elaine and me get your arms over our shoulders, even if it's only for balance, and we can head for the car."

"Yeah, that's good."

Carter had pain as they helped get his arms over their shoulders, but once they were moving, things seemed OK. At the car, they helped Carter slide into the back seat. Once he was in and buckled up, Tom and Elaine took a minute.

"Tom, is that other guy dead?"

"Yeah, I think so. Yeah, he's dead. You OK? I mean are you feeling OK, and, I mean, about him being dead?"

"I'm going to have some bruises and all, but nothing too bad. I don't feel much about that guy being dead. He was going to rape me and I'm pretty sure he was going to kill me. I'm glad he's dead instead of that. Maybe it'll hit me, but not yet. I'm kinda shaky about the whole thing, but not that. He hit you with that tire iron. Aren't you hurt?"

"Like you. I'm gonna have some bruises. But he never hit me solid."

"You're amazing."

The hug and kiss were gentle. However the kiss didn't feel the same to Tom. Although Elaine was warm and soft and close and felt wonderful, those wonderful sensations came to him at a distance from where Tom now found himself.

Elaine handed Tom the car keys. "Can you drive so I can sit in the back with Carter?"

"Whatever you want." He gave her a quick kiss and Elaine slid into the back with Carter. Tom was about to get in when he had a thought. He walked over to the assailants' pick up truck, looked at it and thought. He got his knife again, went to a front tire and went to work on its valve stem. He pulled on it, bent it over and sawed back and forth. It started hissing air, but he kept on until it was completely severed. Tom stood, looked and thought for a second. As the tire rapidly deflated, Tom gained confidence that between their injuries and a flat front tire, it would be some time before they could be in a position to come after them. He climbed behind the wheel of Elaine's car and headed the car toward the highway. On the highway he pushed his speed up, eager to both put the mess at the rest stop behind them and to get Carter to a doctor.

It was a relief to be under way again. Tom tried to think of what he should do, but it was like his brain had stopped working. He basically just drove. The road forward through a tunnel of light became his world.

In the back, Elaine was focused on figuring out how to take care of Carter. Up to this point in her life, she had always been a child. Her parents and in particular her mother had always been the person who took care of things like this. Now it fell to her to be that person – the person she needed to be regardless of what she had always been before, and to do what needed to be done.

As they got closer to Lebanon, Elaine got on her phone to look for a hospital. "It looks like there's a hospital on the far side of Lebanon and one at Dartmouth. I think the one at Dartmouth one is supposed to be good."

Carter responded. "I'm actually feeling pretty decent. Lots better. Maybe we should just go up to New Thetford." His voice was still a bit ragged and hollow, leading Elaine to doubt Carter's assessment of his condition.

Tom roused himself from his mental lethargy. "Yeah, I want to get there too, but they really beat you up. You could be hurt worse than you think."

They debated among themselves for a minute, but ultimately Elaine yielded since everyone, herself included, wanted so much to just be there that they were happy to believe that Carter was basically OK. They pressed on.

The mood in the car shifted when they crossed the river into Vermont. The relief was almost tangible. Still, they were mostly quiet as they exited from 89 onto Route 91 and headed north for the ten minutes or so it took to get to the Route 113 exit. From there Elaine gave Tom directions to her aunt's house.

When they pulled in, the front door light came on. Elaine's aunt came out to greet them. Her uncle hung in the doorway, smiling a greeting.

Tom heaved a sigh as he opened the door. He gathered himself up before boosting himself out. He felt a little light headed and sort of detached from things, although perhaps not quite as badly as he had been. Meanwhile Elaine had climbed out of the back seat and ran to her aunt, bursting into tears as they approached each other. "Aunt Jill, it was terrible!" She shook as she sobbed. Tom ached for her as emotion re-entered his life.

Her aunt gathered Elaine into her arms and comforted her. When Elaine had quieted a little, her aunt asked, "What happened, baby?"

In the meanwhile, her uncle Bill, realizing that there was trouble, went to Tom. As he saw all the blood his eyes grew large. "Are you OK?" his voice making the shock over what he was seeing clear.

"I'm OK. A few bruises. Carter's hurt way worse" glancing at the back seat.

"So that's not your blood then?"

"Nope. Can you give me a hand helping Carter?"

"It's not Carter's blood either?"

"No, they beat him pretty bad, but he isn't bleeding much. It's from the guys who attacked us."

"Well, ah, OK. Ah, let's give Carter a hand then."

Carter had gotten himself unbuckled and had swung his legs out onto the ground. Now he was getting ready to push himself up out of the car.

"Whoa. Hold on just a sec – ah – Carter. Let Tom and me help you."

They all made their way into the house. Aunt Jill fussed with Carter to see that he was not in serious distress. She went and got a wash cloth and cleaned the dirt and blood from the bruises and scrapes on his face, hands and forearms. She poked, prodded, and rubbed him to see if there were any serious hidden injuries. Only when she failed to identify any did she turn to Elaine. "What happened baby?"

Elaine recounted the story. Her aunt and uncle were aghast. "What happened to the other guys?"

"We left them there."

"Did the police help them? What did the paramedics say?"

"No Aunt Jill. We just came here. God, I guess I should have called the police or something. I didn't think. We were going to take Carter to the hospital, but he didn't want to go, so we just came here."

"But they could be hurt badly."

Tom, in a muted voice, interjected. "I think the two who were beating Carter aren't too bad. The other guy – the one who was dragging Elaine – is dead. I'm pretty sure."

There was a long moment of silence. Uncle Bill broke it. "Jill honey, why don't you stay here with the kids. I'll go make some calls."

They talked and a little while later Bill returned. "The police say that someone already called in the three men at the rest area. They're on their way to the hospital. I'm sure they're there by now. The police here are sending someone over and they're sending an ambulance here as well. I called Harvey." and to the kids explained, "He's our lawyer. He promised to come right over."

It was over two hours before things calmed down at the house. All the kids made quick calls home to let their parents know what was going on. When the police arrived they were upset about the situation and the fact that a mess like this had landed in their laps. They immediately took possession of Tom's knife, and they wanted to take all the kids off to jail. The lawyer was having none of that. The police backed off that idea and zeroed in on Tom, at which point Elaine became frantic. The paramedics recommended that they take Carter to the hospital, but he wanted none of that. Things were going badly until a call came in for the police. The more senior trooper took the call outside.

He returned about five minutes later. "My commander has been in touch with the New Hampshire commander in charge of the scene there. I guess they knew the people who attacked you. They're OK with leaving you here until tomorrow when we can sort through this mess. Is that acceptable?"

It was.

"You WILL stay here. You will not leave the state. You won't leave the town. Better that you not leave the premises. Am I understood?"

He was.

"Someone will be in touch in the morning. Have a good

evening." And with that, the first semblance of sanity returned.

Jill insisted that each of the kids call their parents again to fill them in. She and Bill stood by in case they were needed. It was a long half hour before they were able to wrap things up, if only for the night.

That done, Jill set to reorganizing sleeping arrangements. They had planned to have Elaine in their spare room – a small room wedged into the far end of the second floor from the master bedroom – but due to his injuries, the bed went to Carter. Bill went with him to get him up the stairs and settled.

Due to the late hour, Elaine was assigned to the living room couch, which had previously been reserved for Tom. The only other flat space for sleeping was on the floor beside the couch, which suited an exhausted Tom fine. In short order Tom was asleep.

"Tom?"

"Uh."

"Tom?"

"Huh. Yeah. Elaine."

"Tom, can I come down there with you? I can't sleep."

"Sure. Let me slide over."

As she settled down next to him, they kissed and embraced.

"I was afraid."

"You don't have to be. While I'm around no one will ever hurt you."

"I know. I'm not afraid now, close to you." Her hands slid up under his T shirt and caressed him.

He drew her close and his response to her closeness and her touch was immediate. Her hand slide down inside his shorts. A minute later she took his hand and guided it down the front of her sweat pants.

"Tom, let's do it. Let's make love. Now."

Their first time together was awkward at times, but their passion was intense. Far too soon they were complete.

After they had separated, Tom murmured, "Elaine, I love…"

Elaine took her fingers and lay them on his lips. "Shh." Within a minute her breathing had become regular.

Tom lay awake for a while. Despite everything, he found that he was happy. It wasn't long before sleep found him too.

Chapter 19

In the morning, Tom woke to noise from the bathroom. He smiled when he saw Elaine, naked, lying next to him and remembered their lovemaking. Then he realized with a start that they were lying together, naked, on her aunt's living room floor. In the same instant, the terrible events of the previous night crashed back into his consciousness. Tom's breath caught in his throat as he tried to muster words. When he managed to speak, his hushed voice was urgent. "Elaine. Baby. Wake up.

C'mon, wake up."

Her eyes opened, and she smiled, contented. Tom's mind calmed, at least a little, as his heart melted. "Baby. Babe. We have to get up. Get dressed."

She smiled.

"Your aunt and uncle are awake. They're moving around. We need to get dressed."

Now Elaine responded. "Tom. Thank you. For everything. You are wonderful and I love you."

Elaine's words echoed in Tom's mind and as they did, the turmoil there eased, if only a little. As he formed words, a focus started to emerge. "Last night with you was wonderful. So much of it was so awful. Bad. But you're wonderful, and I love you." As the echoes of his own words rang through his mind and mixed with the echoes of Elaine's, the focus continued to grow. The horrors of the previous night were still there and always would be. That was clear. But as he held Elaine, he felt hope for a future he desired.

"Elaine, I love you. But your aunt and uncle are up, and we need to get dressed."

Although she seemed unconcerned, she did as Tom asked. More than once as she dressed languorously and he saw her naked body it was all he could do to keep putting clothes on instead of ripping off both his and hers.

When she finished dressing she walked up to Tom, lay her hands flat on his chest and lay her head next to them. "I liked it when you called me babe."

His hands found their way to her hips. "I like calling you babe. A lot. Babe."

"Big boy."

"I guess!" Tom shifted, trying to relieve the strain on his pants.

"I can help." Her hands crept toward his waist.

"Oh god, how can something as amazing as this be a nightmare?"

Just then the door from the hallway opened. Tom and Elaine parted.

"Who needs the bathroom?"

Tom took the offer and sidled past Jill awkwardly. Elaine started organizing blankets and pillows, folding and putting things away.

The day was pretty crazy. Elaine slowly regained a more normal demeanor, but every time she looked at Tom, she smiled. Tom was less blatant, but still hopelessly smitten by Elaine.

Carter still had plenty of aches and pains, but he was hurting less and able to move better. A night's sleep had done wonders. The bruises on his face had become colorful, which looked pretty odd, but he was on the mend.

Various parents arrived starting just after 10:00. Cam Johnson arrived first, followed shortly after by Grace and Cole. Elaine's family arrived around 11:30. The police had checked in early in the morning, wanting to confirm that the three visitors were still present. A formal meeting had been scheduled for 1:00

PM, although Bill's impression as he'd spoken to them was that there was very little rush. The police seemed most interested in giving the various parents time to arrive and get sorted out. Jill and Bill's lawyer agreed with the parents to represent all three of the victims/persons of interest.

As one o'clock approached, Tom was pretty nervous. His mom tried to reassure him, to little effect. Then his dad took him aside.

"You seem nervous. Jumpy."

"I guess I am. I killed a guy and put two others in the hospital. That isn't good. I could be in big trouble."

"It's possible, but I don't see it. If you were in big trouble, you'd be in jail. It's sort of amazing they didn't take you in. At least put you in jail overnight. It sounds to me like the cops who came here last night were a little freaked out at the idea of what you did. That's what it sounds like to me. But I'm pretty sure that by the time they left they were mostly OK. Sure they read you the riot act about not skipping town. That would be a mess for them. But they don't seem to want to prosecute you. I think it's going to be OK."

"But I killed that guy." Tom's voice was anguished

"May he rest in peace." Cole's voice grew hard. "The piece of shit. He was going to rape Elaine and kill her. You stopped him. The good guy won. End of fucking story." Cole paused. "I know I've said this before, but I am proud of you. That doesn't even begin to say it. On the other hand, you screwed up when you didn't take Carter straight to the hospital and call the police from there. But I get it, and the police did too. As great a job as you did protecting yourself and your friends, this was your first time facing a crazy situation. A terrible thing happened and you were shaken up. You deserve some slack. Just do better if it ever happens again. That's all."

Tom had been calming down as his father laid out his view of things, but the thought of something like that happening again shocked him. "God, I didn't think of that. Something like this could happen again. That's awful."

"Yeah it would be. What would be a hundred times worse would be not dealing with it. Not keeping your head. Not taking control of the situation. Not doing just like you did this time – if it ever comes to it. I know lots of guys would disagree, but I think that's part of being a man. Being strong. Being ready. And with the world going the way it is, you may need to be very strong. I wish it wasn't true, but it is."

Tom straightened his shoulders. It made sense. His determination firmed.

Cole could see it happen before his eyes. It brought a kind of joy – a gift only parents know. His boy, taking another step – a big one – in becoming a man, the kind of good man Cole had always dreamed he would be.

This interview with police had a firmer tone than the meeting with the Boston police, a hundred years before. These police seemed less hard than those in Boston had been, but just as tough, like there was granite in their bones. They reviewed the facts as they saw them, which put Tom and friends in a good light. As the lawyer listened, he saw this as a clear indication that the bad people these young people had overcome were well known to the police, and the police were happy to have them off the streets. When the issue of Tom carrying a deadly weapon came up, Cole asked if he could comment.

"He was carrying that knife on my specific instructions. In fact I sharpened it so my boy – my son – would be ready as best he possibly could be for whatever came his way. I can't tell you how happy I am that I did. He did nothing last night that I hadn't talked to him about and told him to do. If there is any fault there, it's mine."

The senior police official directed a cold glare at Cole, who sat impassively. The moment passed.

It took some time to talk things through, but eventually it was concluded. For the time being, the police had no intention of pressing charges. The investigation would continue until it had run its course. Until it had, Tom in particular was to let the police know where he was and how to get in touch with him.

Afterward, Mr. and Mrs. Inoue took Tom aside. "First of all Tom, from now on, we are Hiro and Manda to you." Manda broke into tears, "Thank you for protecting our little girl. Our young woman. When I saw her I knew – about you two. A mother knows. Lainey and I talked, and she made it clear – you two are together. I guess it was a shock, but no surprise, if you know what I mean. You two are good together and my sweet girl is happy. So am I."

Hiro took up where Manda left off. "Tom. Me too. She's lucky to have a guy like you. If you ever hurt her, I'll kick your ass." Hiro tried for his penetrating glare to drive home the point, but failed completely, and smiled, resigned to his gratitude.

"Maybe you'll understand some day what I mean when I say that. What I'm really saying is just love her. Always. That's all I ask."

"Mr. Inou… uh, Hiro. That's easy. Elaine is wonderful."

Tom glanced over to see Elaine in conversation with his parents. As he watched, his mother smiled, and with tears in her eyes, hugged Elaine. When his father hugged her, he smiled in a way Tom had never seen before. It later struck Tom that it was a little like the way his grandfather smiled at him.

When the hug was complete, Elaine looked over at him and smiled. His heart melted, yet again.

When things wrapped up with the police, Tom and Elaine went for a walk and talked.

"I guess our secret is out, huh."

"Not much of a secret. Mom knew as soon as she saw me. She's fine with it. So is Dad, at least mostly. They both love you."

"What's happening with, ah, sleeping arrangements."

"I guess Mom sorted it out with Aunt Jill and Mr. Johnson. Carter is doing fine, but his dad wants to stay and make sure. They're in the tent. You and I get the guest room."

"Hmm, I feel a nap coming on."

"Control yourself, big boy."

"Whatever you say, babe."

They continued to walk and talk. Tom marveled at the last

twenty four hours – how much had changed. He had no idea how to think about the fight. It didn't bother him. He just didn't know what to make of it, and of himself as a guy who had killed a bad man and sent two more like him to the hospital. All of the terrible and wonderful events of the last day still rattled and reverberated in his mind. The overall effect was unsettling. When the power and focus he brought to the fight the night before came to his mind, his discomfort was intense. When he relived driving a knife into another man's ribcage, it was terrible. There was no glory or goodness in it. However it had been necessary, and as Tom was able to accept that necessity, it gave rise to peace of a sort. Tom did not like it, but found he could embrace it. He could live with it, and that was enough.

However when he combined that with what he and Elaine had discovered in each other, the result was something he had never imagined. It had been wonderful making love to Elaine. Just a day ago he could only dream about living with her – sharing a bed with her. Today he couldn't imagine not lying beside her in bed, loving her. Sharing his life with her. He still felt a little odd about how this changed things with their parents, but couldn't imagine not loving Elaine, in every sense of the word.

"Oh, uh, Tom. I guess that we need to try to be, uh, quieter, you know. I guess Aunt Jill and Uncle Bill were, uh, aware that we needed a little privacy this morning."

"Oops." They looked at each other and laughed, a bit embarrassed. They would try to be quieter as they got to know each other in a new way.

They headed back. On the way, discussion shifted to plans going forward. Tom suggested, "Let's stay for a while and help with the New Thetford project, if they'll let us. I'd like to help out and get to know more about the project. Sorta' like you did last summer."

"Sure. I'd like that. Maybe we'll know more after our tour tomorrow morning."

"Maybe. I just wonder if a project like this would want some high school kids getting in the way."

"Tom, I don't think you're giving yourself enough credit. Or me either. Or Carter."

"Well they know you, and you worked here last summer. They don't know Carter and me at all."

"Well let's not worry about it. It won't help anything. But I have faith in you. And Carter too."

"If it does come together, do you think we can stay with Jill and Bill for a while?"

"I'll ask. I think so, probably. They like me and you're kind of a hero."

Tom looked at her funny.

"You are. You saved me. And Carter too."

Tom scowled. Elaine playfully poked him in the ribs. He wrapped an arm around her and pulled her close. She melted into him.

When they arrived back at the house dinner was almost ready.

Everyone else had pitched in to make it, and Tom and Elaine became the targets of good-natured teasing about perfect timing for having missed the dinner prep.

Dinner was pretty much perfect. Good simple food, wonderful people, and a Vermont setting that could never be described properly, only experienced. Jill and Bill's house was almost at the base of Cobble Hill. To the east lay the Connecticut River and the hills in New Hampshire. To the north you looked up river toward East Thetford, another 'don't blink or you'll miss it' Vermont crossroads. To the west was Cobble Hill, with its impressively steep east slope. To the south, when you looked down river toward White River Junction, you could just see the edge of the New Thetford construction project peeking around the corner of Cobble Hill's gentler south slope. Pretty much perfect.

Talk mostly stayed away from the drama in New Hampshire, instead focusing on the New Thetford project. Tom and Carter had heard so much about the project and were aching to see it, tantalized by the corner of it they could see a half mile away. Their excitement and Elaine's enthusiasm were contagious.

After dessert was finished, neighbors started wandering by. Most of them knew Elaine a little from previous visits, and they gravitated toward her, which led to introductions to Tom and Carter. It quickly became obvious that the three of them were the attraction for the visitors, having heard about both their work on their climate adaptation project and their misadventure en route to Thetford.

Carter excused himself early. He was mostly OK, but not completely recovered, and wanted to get a good night's sleep before going to the New Thetford construction site the next day. Cam went with him. After that, things unwound pretty quickly. Not quickly enough for Elaine and Tom's preferences, though. Soon they excused themselves, using the same excuse about wanting to be ready for the next day. Despite the excuse, it was some time before they slept.

To no one's surprise, Tom and Elaine were not up early. When they emerged from their room they wound up having to skip breakfast and hustle to make it to the site by eight. Jill thrust some raisin bread toast, dripping with melted butter, into their hands as they exited the house.

They hustled as they made their way to the site. Carter, still somewhat sore, his face now very colorful from his many bruises, struggled to keep up. Once there, they asked around for Sean, their contact. They were directed to the site office, which occupied the corner of the new construction that had been the first bit to be finished. They had to wait a few minutes while he finished figuring out the next round of work with a crew. When that was done, he came out of his office, a hardhat on his head and three more in his hands for them. "Let's take a walk." When Elaine put her hard hat on, Tom decided it made her look incredibly sexy.

Everyone introduced themselves as they made their way toward the center of the construction project. That done, Sean continued. "So Tom, you worked construction with your dad last summer? He's a carpenter?"

"Yep, he is. A contractor. I worked full time last summer and part time the summer before."

"You swept a lot of floors."

"Ayup."

Sean laughed. "You're sounding like a Vermonter already. What else did you do?"

"Mostly I was a laborer type. I did use all the regular tools on the site. Did quite a bit of framing – both advanced wall framing and conventional. Drove truck a little, but nothing big. I did most of the computer stuff. Just a little bit of CAD too."

"And you've been using hand tools ever since you can remember."

"Pretty much."

"Are you any good at any of it?"

"Not as good as my dad, except on the computer, but that's not saying much – he's hopeless on computers. By the end of the summer I was holding my own most days with the carpentry, except when I screwed up. And I sweep floors real good."

As they walked around the site, Sean explained how one big part of the project was to minimize their impacts on the earth, with special emphasis on minimizing impacts on fertile land, and how those priorities dictated a large part of New Thetford's design and construction processes.

"Elaine, I think I remember from last summer that you're interested in gardening and agroforestry. Do I have that right?"

"Yeah, that was the kind of stuff I was working on with my aunt. But I want to learn it all."

Sean beamed a smile at her. "Well I hope you live to be really old, 'cause that could take awhile. But in the meanwhile, it works for me. We're trying to do sort of an internship program. We need to get this place built, but a big priority is getting people experienced with everything that goes into creating a radically efficient community. From here, we want our interns to be able to spread out to help build lots more RECs like New Thetford. The idea is you learn the basics of a bunch of things before you focus on anything specific. If you're interested, it means you sweep a lot of floors and work as a go'fer until we can trust you to be safe on the construction site. You'll get hands-on exposure to several trades. You can also try out other work that goes into creating a new community, but most of the work at this stage of the game is in construction. If you're going to work on creating new communities, you have to be safe and useful on construction sites."

As they continued their walk, Sean explained how the New Thetford project primarily used a blend of pole barn and frame and plank styles of construction. "The pole barn part is where we use small individual footings to support stub columns that then support the structural frames. We use the small individual footings to minimize impacts on the soil. Perimeter footings are incredibly tough on soil, and if you add concrete slabs, its 'game over' for soil bugs, so we avoid concrete whenever we can."

Sean's comments about soil health caught Elaine's ear. "That's really great that people are thinking about how construction techniques affect soil health. I never would have thought about buildings' foundations from that perspective."

"You and most other people, too. It's been great for me learning to think differently about all this stuff – stuff that I've always taken for granted. Anyway, once we have a line of footings topped with the right height of a column stub to make it all level, we set a line of floor beams on top of them. Once we have two lines of beams in place, we tie them together with our versions of 'planks'. Mill style construction like you have down in the Merrimack Valley mostly used three inch thick planks. We use wooden 'I' beams that we put together here, instead of traditional planks. Their top surfaces double as subfloor and we usually attach ceilings to the bottom surfaces. When we're ready to finish an area, we add finish flooring, which ties it all together. But all the finish stuff happens after we put a roof on it to avoid damage when it rains.

"Back to the first section of floor we put in. After the first bay of the new building is decked, that crew goes on and starts planking the next bay right on the heels of the guys doing the floor beams. At the same time the regular framing crew gets to work on framing the next story. Working on a decent floor with standardized components makes it go even faster than the foundations and stub columns. We add bracing to stiffen it up as we go. As soon as the first two sections are framed in, another planking crew starts work on the second floor."

Tom was totally focused as Sean explained about this new way to build buildings. From his work in Newburyport, Tom was pretty knowledgeable about stick built construction, and there had been no avoiding some exposure to post and beam construction. As Sean dug into the details of frame and plank construction, Tom's mind wandered to the old mills across the

Merrimack River in Amesbury and in all of the old mill towns further upriver.

"At that point everything goes into high gear. One crew goes along adding more structural frames on the first floor, followed by the planking team. When the second bay is done, another crew starts adding frames and then floors on top of floor one. At that point a new batch of teams gets going on roughing in walls, stairs, heat, sprinklers, plumbing and stuff like that. Before you know it we're putting a greenhouse on top of the whole thing to serve as a roof and to create somewhere we can grow greens in the winter and raise warm-climate crops, especially perennials. Up to that point, everything is really standardized and really fast.

"As the greenhouse crew gets moving along, crews to build walls and interior spaces start. That stuff isn't as standardized and moves a little slower. Still, we keep everything as standardized as we can."

As Sean led them to their next stop, he discussed the pros and cons of post and beam construction versus frame and plank construction and pointed out a few places where they had used extra beams to supplement the structure.

"Now here you can see how we deal with the spaces between buildings. Our idea is to keep the spacing between columns standardized across the whole construction site, as much as we can. We space columns at 14 feet 9 'cuz that's pretty exactly four and a half meters. That way it's easy to make changes later on – to make one building bigger and another building smaller. Stuff like that. It means that the spaces between buildings are smaller than ordinary roads, although they would be big enough for one way traffic, at least if we weren't on a hillside.

"The walls we build on each side of the gap have really good fire ratings. The same for all the outside walls of buildings. That way we can limit the spread of any fire. That plus sprinklers everywhere and we figure we're pretty safe from from fire."

As they paused at the far end of the current construction, Carter commented. "I like that you're paying so much attention to fire. Fire is a scary thing. We had a neighbor down the road – a friend of my dad – who lost a barn and lots of livestock to a fire four years ago. It was a big part of the reason his farm went out." Carter's earnest expression highlighted his interest.

"That had to have been sad. Losing a barn is bad, but losing livestock is worse. So Carter, do I understand you're a farm kid?"

"I was until the farm failed."

"Sorry to hear that Carter. You're from the Midwest maybe, judging from your accent?"

"Yes sir."

Sean smiled. "Carter, the name is Sean. I'm just a woodchuck from Vermont, and prone to get confused if people call me 'sir'."

"OK, uh, Sean."

"Where were we? Right, you were a farm kid from the Midwest. What happened?"

Rough Road

"Well, around Bismark, in North Dakota, we had some really bad weather. Things on the farm were bad and then my mom died. She kind of ran the business and my dad took care of growing vegetables. He was good at that, but not the business end of things, if you know what I mean."

"I'm really sorry about your mother. Had to be hard." Sean walked a little before continuing. "I do know what you're talking about – how some people are good growing crops. Others are good with business stuff. They're different things, and no one is good at everything." Sean looked over at Elaine with a mischievous smile. "Of course since Elaine wants to learn it all, which I have no doubt she will manage to do, she will no doubt be the exception that proves the rule. Of course she may be kind of old by that point." He grinned.

"Good thing that the women in the Inoue family live to be really, really old." Elaine grinned right back at Sean.

"Elaine, you're gonna fit right in here if you aren't careful. So Carter, did you help out on the farm?"

"Sure, especially as I got older and things got harder. Dad tried to keep it down – my work load – but I worked a couple of hours every day and more on weekends."

"What are you good at?"

"I did OK with things. My dad has a better sense about what growing things need. I mean I understand the basics, but he has a gift. I'm better than my dad at keeping the equipment running. And computers."

"Which end of a hammer do you hold?"

"Depends on what you're doing with it," whereupon Carter snagged a hammer from a nearby table and brandished it, using the appropriate grip on the correct end of the tool.

"Carter, you just may have what it takes."

As they toured the site, they talked more about how framing was modified to adjust its distance closer to or farther from the hill's surface. The point was to keep it close to, but clear of the ground. If the adjustments were vertical, short ramps connected floors beside one another that were at different elevations. If the adjustments were lateral, floor elevations remained the same at the expense of changing the regular rectangular spacing of columns.

Elaine's interest in soil science was apparent when she asked, "So, what *does* happen to the soil under the buildings."

Sean admitted that it wasn't good, "but we figure that as long as we keep toxic materials out of the buildings it'll be tough for them to accumulate in the soil. That's our big focus. We have people working on what kinds of tradeoffs we should be making between keeping the buildings dry and sound but with enough moisture in the soil to support life. It's a work in progress."

As they wrapped up the tour Sean asked, "Any questions?"

It was pretty clear that Sean had to get back to other things, so they answered 'no', despite having a million questions.

"OK, when can you start?"

The three looked at one another, surprise showing on their faces. "It sounds amazing and all but we didn't know, like, this was a job interview." Elaine cringed inwardly at her lame response.

"So you'd all like to work here?" They all agreed enthusiastically. "So the question is simple then. When can you start?"

They looked at each other, incredibly excited, and, led by Tom, responded with various forms of "Now!"

"OK then. Let's start the paperwork."

When they were done, they got an hour for lunch, and made a bee line for Jill and Bill's house. When they burst in the door, Elaine headed for the kitchen to make sandwiches with Carter close behind to assist. Explaining was delegated to Tom.

Tom headed to the living room where everyone else was gathered. "They hired us!"

Everyone was excited for them, with the exception of Cole, who congratulated them just like the rest, but Tom could tell his heart wasn't in it. Then Tom realized what he had done. He went over to his father.

"Dad, I got so excited and everything, I didn't even think about working with you this summer. I'm sorry."

"Don't be. You're doing the right thing. This is a special place. A great place, and it's a great time to do this. I'm not going to lie – I like having you around. But it couldn't be clearer. You're doing the right thing. As much as I want you working with me, I want you working here more. I guess it's a dad thing."

Tom was still feeling bad. "Dad. I feel kinda dumb. I shoulda' known how you would feel."

"Well OK, maybe it was a little dumb. But like I've told you a hundred times, you're the smartest dumbass I've ever known."

"It's probably more like a thousand times by now, Dad. At least now you can take Tony back on. I was feeling pretty bad about that. He needs the job."

"What are they paying you?"

"I'd make more working for you. Lots more."

"Benefits?"

"Pretty good. As good as you."

"So maybe you aren't such a smart dumbass, but you're happy. And you're right about Tony. Anyway I am happy for you, which means just plain happy, being your dad and all. A few regrets, sure. But happy. Now go eat."

"Twist my arm."

Elaine looked the question at him when he came over. He nodded back that he'd tell her later. She smiled and his heart melted.

At the end of the day, they dragged themselves home. Tom actually wasn't bad, but the other two were beat. Elaine had worked up a large blister from pushing the broom. Even though he was on light duty until he was cleared by a doctor, Carter collapsed in proper teen fashion. For him the problem was really more the left over effects of the beating than the day's work. No one else was there, but Tom figured they would all be back for dinner.

They all drank a couple of glasses of water as they laid atop chairs and the couch. "OK guys, we need to go buy decent boots, gloves, hard hats and eye protection." Tom knew the drill on job sites.

"But they gave us everything except the boots."

"Elaine. The gloves are crap, the hard hat suspension sucks and you're going to want a sweat band with it, and the eye protection is uncomfortable. Only dorks wear that shit."

"Oh." Elaine smiled sweetly at Tom, which told him, clear as day, that he was going to hear about his little declaration later. He sighed happily.

Carter added his non-committal grunt, acknowledging the inevitability of whatever it was Tom had said.

Elaine got on her phone to her aunt, who was still at work. She directed them to where they could find stores to provide them the new essentials. They reluctantly pried themselves from their comfortable positions of collapse and headed for Elaine's car. "'Hop in the car and...'. It's the American way."

The guys agreed with Elaine. "Cars suck." was Carter's contribution. He added, "We need to figure out a better way."

Elaine was upbeat. "We're working on it at least."

Tom wanted to know, "Is there a neighborhub planned for New Thetford?" No one knew. "We'll have to check it out. Then we could order stuff on line and get it delivered right there fast and free."

They hurried through the stores. Even so, they were a little late for dinner and utterly starved. Everyone else was waiting for them before eating.

Dinner was pleasant again, but a little sad. Cole, Grace and Hiro had to get back to work, and although his boss had told Cam to take whatever time he needed to take care of his son, he felt it was smart to get back to work sooner rather than later. After all, Carter was upright and hurting less after an afternoon's work on a construction site than before – a good sign. All of which meant that tonight was the last time any of the three would see their immediate families for some time, and they were all feeling odd about it.

Eventually eight o'clock rolled around and Cole declared, "I guess it's that time."

"I'm glad we're caravanning with you." Manda shuddered as she thought of what had nearly happened to their daughter.

Tom wasn't worried. He was certain that his dad had his 1911 . 45 semi-auto in the truck and had complete confidence that he knew how to use it. His father had seen action in the Army before he and his mom were married, and knew what it took to win when things got violent. On the other hand it would be a slow trip back since his father was always extra careful when he was carrying. If he got stopped, the chances of trouble from nervous police were much higher when you had a weapon with you.

One more time, hugs were shared and kisses bestowed, and then their families were gone, leaving all three of them feeling a little empty.

That evening when Tom and Elaine went to bed, Elaine was a little teary, feeling the separation from her family more than she had earlier. They made love and then lay beside one another for a while and drifted off. However it wasn't long before Tom was wakened by Elaine's hands exploring his body and then finding what she had been looking for. Pleased with herself, she murmured "big boy" in his ear, in her new, crazy sexy voice.

In the morning, Tom was the first one up and rousted the others. "C'mon, we need to get up. We need food, and we need to get out the door. Trust me, it'd be a bad idea to be late for work on our first full day." Their breakfast was rushed and they had to hustle on the way to the site, but did manage to arrive at 7:00 exactly to get their first assignments for the day.

At the end of the day, they were all thankful it was Friday. Although everyone has a crazy week every now and then, crazy weeks like theirs were, thankfully, pretty much unheard of. Lots of the craziness had been good, but none of it was easy. They needed a weekend badly.

Chapter 20

On Friday they had been invited by some of their co-workers to come along to the Pomp (which translated to 'the Ompompanoosuc River' to 'outatownahs') to go swimming. It sounded great to all three of them.

As it turned out, it was. The river was beautiful, although the water was still cold. However with the bright sun and warm air it all worked out fine. Tom and Elaine mostly hung out together, Tom finding her skimpy two piece bathing suit incredibly sexy. Others would wander by and talk, or Tom and Elaine would jump in the water and meet new people as they lazed about and explored the swimming hole. Carter's many bruises were still on display, but at least were starting to fade a little. He made some new friends and spent most of the day hanging with them. All three of the new transplants were surprised at how many people wanted to hear more about their Nousamont community project, and wound up having some good conversations about it.

People also talked about news from the world. The biggest topic was the growing backup of climate refugees trying to get into Canada. Canada had been burned by the Americans who were actually refugees but lied about it to enter the country. In response, Canada tightened up the border, with the result that small refugee camps were growing near ports of entry. They became the homes of people who had nowhere in particular to go and believed that Canada was the best place to build a future. A couple of the camps in Vermont weren't even that small any more, especially at the crossings in Highgate and Derby at Routes 89 and 91. To everyone's concern, the camps were growing at an increasing rate. The word was that Vermont wasn't prepared for lots of climate refugees, which left people wondering what was going to happen.

The other big topic was the ever-growing list of climate disasters around the country and the world. This year's tornadoes, at least in the US, weren't bad by new standards for catastrophic weather, but by historical standards they were terrible. Some areas were very dry, and elsewhere there was flooding. The pushes toward regenerative agriculture and horticulture were huge. Everyone at the swimming hole was happy about that.

A few climate adaptation businesses were doing great – inoculant-grade cold compost companies were booming everywhere, and a couple of startup ultralight rail companies had settled on some standards for track gauge, rail cross sections, electronic navigation, control protocols, and other essential bits for sane standardization of this new transportation mode.

At the end of the day, bicycling back to New Thetford on their borrowed bikes was a mixed experience. It had been a wonderful day, but they all had sunburns and even their light shirts were irritating. Plus, it had cooled off enough for their tender skins to chill as they pedaled along.

They had already checked in via phone with Bill and Jill to let them know they had been invited to have dinner with new friends. They stopped at the house to grab some soft, warm clothing and to pick up a side dish that Bill had been kind enough to put together for their pot luck.

Dinner was nice. It was another beautiful evening. The only unpleasant distraction was the news about the hack attack on smart cars earlier in the day. It had been stopped after only a hundred or so people had been targeted and run down by empty cars. The good news was that this attack was nowhere near as bad as several previous ones. As people talked about it, they agreed that the only genuinely bright side to new technology for personal transportation was with ultralight rail, in part because of its lower vulnerability to such attacks. The new protocols being adopted for the emerging generation of ultralight rail tech promised even better protection than the inherent advantage of railways – that as long as you aren't standing on the rail way itself, you are safe from rogue rail vehicles. The people at the party were proud that legislation to replace all roads with ultralight railways had passed in Vermont's just-finished session, even though it would be years before the transition was complete.

Although they were enjoying their new friends, Tom and Elaine were tired so they excused themselves early and headed home to bed. Quite a bit later as he was finally surrendering to sleep, Tom marveled at Elaine's enthusiasm for their lovemaking. Earlier in the evening there had been a couple of false starts at sleep, but each time, Elaine had recovered and through gentle but resolute encouragement, roused Tom yet again. Thinking how this was all a dream come true, Tom joined Elaine in sleep.

In the morning there was a message from Carter, who had crashed at the house of a new friend. They were thinking about doing some biking and hiking and invited Tom and Elaine to come along. Looking at the time stamp on the message – in the wee hours of the morning – they had a leisurely breakfast before messaging back that they wanted to go along, and asked when and where they would meet. Then they went back to bed for a while.

By the end of the day they knew Cobble Hill a lot better, as well as some of the other beautiful areas around New Thetford. That evening as they sat around the house, Carter broached the idea of inviting Mace to come up and join them. "If you guys are OK with it, I'll talk to Sean to see whether he would like to talk to Mace. If Sean is interested and things work out, Mace and I could share an apartment."

Elaine and Tom were fine with it. Mace and Elaine had been the two really smart members of Team Carbon, and Tom knew that Mace was pretty handy with tools from a project Grady Construction had done for the Carters where Mace had pitched in. They all figured he would be a good addition.

When Monday rolled around, Tom marveled that work felt normal – a normal that he really liked. He was learning a lot about timber framing and the specific ways they were doing it in New Thetford. To Tom it felt almost like the framing crew was working with a kids' toy construction set – a really big toy construction set. With standard columns, beams, and structural flooring assemblies made of wood that mostly all just fit together, it could hardly have been less complicated. They had to custom cut bracing to reinforce offsets between floors and in a few other situations, but mostly everything was standardized. Construction flew.

One effect of this was that spaces for new housing units opened up on a daily basis. As members of the construction crew, they were entitled to priority access to housing. However, most of the spaces went to Vermonters who wanted out of remote, isolated homes, especially in flood-prone areas. Those vacated homes were mostly being rented to climate refugees.

However the rate of construction at New Thetford created a

problem – the local economy was hard put to create jobs for all the new arrivals. For years Vermont had been trying to generate population growth, but this kind of crazy fast growth brought with it tough challenges. With some help from the state, a new glass manufacturing business was setting up shop in White River Junction, which created some jobs. The big hope for people who paid attention to such things was the high rate at which innovative new businesses were setting up shop in and around New Thetford, mostly in response to the emerging needs of radically efficient communities. They were becoming a big part of building New Thetford both in the literal sense of construction, but also in creating a new economy that held out hope for a new kind of genuine economic sustainability for the country and maybe even the world. It also helped that construction at New Thetford was dead cheap.

Chapter 21

Just after 2:00 PM that afternoon, Carter, Elaine and Tom were on break with the rest of the crew that was setting foundation piers for the newest building when Lillie Stiers, one of the more experienced members of the crew, checked her news feed.

"What the fuck? What the FUCK!"

Since Lillie was one of the quieter, calmer members of the crew, her outburst immediately got everyone's attention. Silence descended.

Elaine, sitting next to Lillie, was the first to respond. "Lillie, what happened?"

Lillie, eyes wide and an astonished expression on her face, looked up from her phone and responded to Elaine. "They just closed our borders. The the governor just closed Vermont's borders to climate refugees!"

A stunned silence fell. Slowly, as others gathered their wits, cell phones came out and people started checking out the news. As they and people across the New Thetford site and the rest of the state did the same thing, the internet feed slowed to a crawl.

Over the coming minutes, the story emerged. The governor of Vermont had just announced plans to limit access into Vermont for climate refugees, effective immediately. He explained that Vermont was caught in the middle between large and growing numbers of people heading north to escape the devastation caused by climate change as southern areas became too hot and more importantly, too dry to sustain traditional agriculture. These farm failures devastated one of the foundational elements of many regional economies. As farms collapsed, devastation cascaded through other parts of the economy. Most victims found ways to get by. Those who couldn't went in search of ways to live.

Refugees from coastal flooding added to the flow of climate refugees. The prediction that the coming hurricane season was going to be a bad one made it even worse.

The greater magnitude of the crisis in Vermont was mostly due to three things. First, the federal government wasn't doing much to help the refugees in the camps on the Canadian border.

Given enough time, Washington could often sort out reasonably simple problems. Unfortunately this problem was anything but simple, and it was happening fast.

The second problem was that Vermont had two major crossings into Canada. Climate refugees were being funneled to large crossings since the many tiny crossings had no way to accommodate and manage refugees stuck on the Canadian border. In Vermont this included not only all the tiny crossings in Vermont but also New Hampshire, which had no large crossings, and almost half of Maine, since the only large crossings in Maine were on its eastern border, hundreds of miles from Vermont. Not only that, but few climate refugees were heading for those crossings in eastern Maine since they were much farther away and led to sparsely populated areas of Canada.

Finally, Vermont was a tiny state, with a tiny economy. The impacts of the refugees on a big state would have been challenging, but to a tiny state, they were ruinous – an immediate threat to the solvency of the state. This combination of circumstances left Vermont straining to cope with a crisis that was growing every day.

Refugees as well as many Vermonters were shocked to think that many ordinary Americans were now being denied access into Vermont. The crew's break ran long that afternoon before the crew chief told people to put their phones away and to get back to work. It was a distracted crew that went back to digging holes, setting pads, and all the rest of it that afternoon. Over the coming days, related stories dominated the news, and little else was discussed by Vermonters and a great many others across the US.

Chapter 22

On Thursday, Tom and Elaine got word that their apartment space was available. And space was all it was. There were no walls – nothing really except for the toilet, shower and basic plumbing that sat in the entirely open and featureless floor space they had been allocated. As members of the construction crew receiving a special benefit, they would have to take on their own build out. Fortunately, prefabbed wall panels, closets, book cases and other ways to quickly create functional walls were available. They wouldn't own any of it – at first anyway – not until they became eligible for the sweat equity program.

What they *would* have was a nice, finished space of their own within a couple of weeks, although with Carter and other friends helping they had enclosed the bathroom and bedroom by noon on Saturday. Tom and Elaine spent Saturday afternoon moving their meager possessions in, along with bits of furniture and furnishings begged and borrowed from friends. They hosted their first dinner party that evening to thank everyone who had helped them.

It appeared that Carter would have his own space soon, and if Mace was able to join them, he and Carter could get an upgrade. Life was good.

Chapter 23

Word from Carter at the end of the day on Monday was that Sean was happy to review an application from Mace promptly if one appeared. Sean was happy with the three new employees he had from Newburyport, which resulted in a favorable predisposition toward Mace. Carter was excited.

A couple of days later Carter let them know that Mace had gotten his application in. At lunch on Friday, Carter told them that Sean had invited Mace up for an interview.

Just over a week later on Sunday the three friends headed out to Lebanon to welcome Mace. They had arranged for a ride to Lebanon to meet him, but were let off on the Vermont side at the West Lebanon bridge to walk across because the driver didn't want to deal with what was happening on the far side of the river.

When they walked across, they were amazed at the crowds of people massed around even the small bridge, which they had been told was nothing compared to the number of people waiting at the highway bridge to get across. They were seeing a result of Vermont's border closure with their own eyes and were amazed and troubled by what they saw.

They were early, so they walked around West Lebanon for a while, and were waiting at the terminal when the bus rolled in. The bus had stuff loaded on racks front and back since lots of passengers these days were carrying a lot with them. Mace's load included his own bike and those belonging to the other three as well. The plan was to load the pile of stuff Mace had brought with him onto their bikes and ride back to New Thetford. When Mace climbed down off the bus, he was greeted with a firm handshake from Tom and hugs from Elaine and Carter. They talked for a couple of minutes while they organized bicycles and gear, but it wasn't long before they were on the road, with the last few items clinging to the bicycles thanks to the roll of duct tape Carter had thought to bring.

Carter and Mace were faster than Elaine, so they led the procession back. When Carter and Mace had opened up a gap between them, Elaine looked over at Tom. "I had been wondering about that."

"Wondering about what?"

"You mean you hadn't noticed?"

Just slightly annoyed with Elaine's coyness, he grumped. "Noticed what?"

"They're gay."

"What are you talking about?"

"Carter and Mace are gay and there's a romance brewing."

"No way."

"Yes, way. And what's wrong with that?"

"Well. I mean there's nothing wrong with that. But Mace and I are friends."

"Yeah, what's your point?"

"Uh. I would know."

"Would you?"

They pedaled for awhile.

"Maybe not, I guess."

"So you'll be cool when and if they come out?"

They pedaled for awhile.

"I'm always cool. I thought you knew that about me. But yeah, I'll be cool."

They pedaled for awhile.

"Good. And yes, you're cool." Elaine continued on in her new and very sexy, naughty voice. "But I kinda like of the hot parts too, big boy." The smile that accompanied the comment definitely gave Tom some ideas.

They rode north along the river on the New Hampshire side. There was another smaller group of refugees at the East Thetford bridge. The vibe as they made their way to the bridge was unpleasant – the people stuck on the border in Lyme were every bit as unhappy about their situations as people downriver.

When they got to the bridge gate, Tom greeted Ted, one of the bridge guards who he knew from swimming expeditions to the Pomp. Ted was expecting them, but with crowds of unhappy people watching, he made a point of checking the list, where he did find their names. As they pedaled into Vermont and homeward, they felt sorry for both the refugees and for their friends tasked with controlling access to Vermont.

After a nice welcome dinner that night in Tom and Elaine's mostly-finished apartment, they hung out until it was time to get to bed. Carter and Mace shared Carter's tent that night, which was pitched in a cleared area not far from Tom and Elaine's apartment. Elaine and Tom made an effort to give them their privacy, just in case.

The next morning Mace's interview with Sean went well, so when lunch time came, the four of them got together to celebrate Mace's hiring. Thanks to Elaine's foresight, they had a picnic. Tom got the job of lugging a large and heavy box containing food and picnic paraphernalia to a beautiful spot on top of the hill that overlooked the surrounding area.

Over the next several days as Carter and Mace relaxed with each other and the people around them, it became pretty clear that the romance was on. The following weekend on Saturday morning before they headed out on another swimming expedition – this time on their own bicycles – Carter and Mace took Elaine and Tom aside and explained that they were a couple. Elaine was cool. And somewhat to the surprise of both Elaine and himself, Tom was too.

Chapter 24

They all had a great summer. They had some crazy weather – rainy stretches and dry ones, some small outbreaks of pests and crop diseases. But the fields around New Thetford handled it all. The crops all did well, thanks to the healthy soil grown by

Thetford-area farmers over the previous thirty years.

Elaine had managed to make her own contribution to New Thetford's soil health initiatives. It turned out that Sean's discussion about construction foundation systems during their initial tour of the site had gotten Elaine thinking. The result was her own project to help figure out the right amount of water to add to the soil beneath New Thetford. When she and Tom had gotten their apartment, she arranged to have their bathroom sink drain directly to a swale she dug in the crawlspace beneath the bathroom. Ever since she had been regularly monitoring the results. Her efforts had sparked enough interest that over the last month she had been asked to dig several more crawlspace swales and had worked with the plumbers to drain some other sinks into them. As each installation was completed, Elaine started monitoring them too. Although it was a small thing, both the soil health team and Sean were impressed by her initiative and perseverance in getting the project going, as well as her reliability in monitoring the soil conditions in and around her swales.

However, news from around the world was getting worse. Old wars continued and a couple of new ones had sprung up. Famine stalked the world. Deadly diseases of people, animals, and plants spread rapidly to areas where they had never been seen before, bringing widespread suffering. The UN again revised its population projection downward. However this time, for the first time in its history, the UN was predicting a decline in the world's population – shocking news for everyone. And much to the concern of people in New Thetford, the situation on Vermont's borders festered.

Chapter 25

Over the summer each of the four newbies had grown in different directions. Tom was really good on the construction and construction planning side of things, proving once again he was his father's son. He did well enough with other work he tried out too (although he was not god's gift to farming – strong and willing is a good start, but good farmers are that and a lot more).

Elaine was good with a wide variety of planning tasks and a very talented farmer. She was getting stronger, which helped with all kinds of things on various work sites. Tom also really liked her increasingly buff body, but that was a side benefit. She was not a natural with construction or mechanical systems, but on the bright side, she never had to be told anything twice.

In terms of job skills and talents, Mace was much like Elaine, but with more muscles. However he proved to be somewhat mercurial in his interests, and not especially reliable. When he was engaged and focused, he was a great addition to a job, but consistency was not his strong point.

Carter was probably the best all-around worker. There seemed to be nothing he couldn't do. On most tasks he was not the single most talented person of the small group, with one significant exception. He was a mechanical wizard. He could fix anything. He rarely needed much by way of parts or supplies to accomplish minor miracles.

One interesting project – repurposing surplus snow making

equipment from ski areas to prevent frost damage to crops – had been languishing until he joined it. Farm crews around Thetford were frequently faced with one of the harsh realities of global warming – that just because the world was getting warmer on the average did not mean that farmers could trust that late frosts would not devastate their crops. In fact, it had become a much worse problem as global climate change progressed.

In no time Carter had a pilot snow making project up and running. Fruit farmers and others with cold snap-sensitive crops were elated. After that, Carter was frequently called in to consult on new installations throughout the area. His talent was much appreciated and his reputation as a mechanical wizard grew.

Chapter 26

In late August Sean took Tom aside. "Tom, I've got a new job for you if you're interested."

Tom's curiosity was piqued. "Whatcha got?"

"Something different. Something pretty new. Actually, totally new is more like it."

Tom's curiosity had him leaning forward, sitting on the edge of his seat. Sean continued. "We're going to be sending a couple of teams out to scout sites for a string of new communities up and down the Connecticut River – two people going each way.

You'd be bicycling."

"That sounds pretty interesting."

"There's more. First, you would be the junior member of one of the parties – either north or south. We are kinda hoping you would go north, since it's a bigger job. The idea is to identify good building sites near every bridge crossing the Connecticut. Everyone – well mostly everyone – agrees we need to find ways to accommodate more people in Vermont. We need to do our part in dealing with the climate migration, but we also need to have more help on hand in case we need to defend the border."

The implications of that took a moment to sink in. "It's that bad at the border now?"

"Nothing good about it, and it's still getting worse."

When Tom didn't respond, Sean continued. "The plan is that, if you want to go north, you'll go with Horst von Neufeld." Tom nodded. He knew Horst from the construction crews. He was a fine craftsman and a hard worker with a reputation for being smart. "You and Horst would be inducted into a new Vermont Militia so you would have official status. Do you know how to handle a gun? A handgun?"

Tom's eyebrows rose. "I've done some shooting with my dad – his 1911.45, and his Glock G31 – a .357 magnum."

Sean's eyebrows rose. "Very good. From what I've heard, you can take care of yourself, even without a gun, but since there is some danger along the border these days, the new Militia will be armed while on duty. For you that would pretty much mean starting when you leave and ending when you get back."

"How long would we be out?"

"Good question. No one really knows. There are fifteen river crossings and at least one primary site to investigate at each one. The south survey team will skip Lebanon but add the Route 91 entry between Bernardston, Mass, and Guilford. No one thinks you can do it all in a week. Some people figure it'll take a month. Most people think it'll take two weeks if everything goes well."

"Who's going to take care of the Lebanon crossings, and the other crossings into Massachusetts, and into New York for that matter." Tom left the obvious comment about everything going well unsaid.

"I'm going to head up the team for Lebanon. We're also going to involve state officials from Montpelier and Concord since it's both big and accessible. We might even have some feds show up, although there are mixed feelings about that. We're not sure about the other little crossings into Mass, but everyone agrees that they have to get done. The New York crossings are a good question, especially since the best guess is that there are more people crossing out of Vermont at them than in. Other questions?"

"I'll need to talk to Elaine."

"Yup. Why don't you and Elaine take the rest of the day to get that started. We'll need your answer soonish."

When he and Sean were done talking, Tom went to find Elaine. He found her sweeping an area where a floor for a bay had just been finished. Tom admired the spectacular view while he waited for her to finish. Once in a while he would also take his eyes off of Elaine to look down at the river and the surrounding fields and hills, which looked pretty nice too.

As Tom and Elaine walked and talked, the feeling grew that this job marked the end of a wonderful time for them. It didn't take them long to agree that Tom should go, but Elaine wanted to talk it all through. She hated the idea of Tom going into any kind of danger. Some tears were shed. She hated the idea of not being with Tom. Some kisses were shared. Tom hated that idea too, and some more kisses were shared. There was some tension as they returned to their apartment, but not between them. It was more a kind of tension – a challenge – that bound them together in a new way, making their relationship stronger.

The next morning, Tom told Sean that he was good to go. After that was done, Tom and Elaine spread the word to friends. The word was already out about the trips, and when they heard that Tom was going, people were pleased. By noon both teams were set. Then word came that the Governor would come down to Thetford the following day to swear them in and wish them well. They would leave early the day after tomorrow.

After lunch, both of the survey teams were assigned to spend the rest of the day and as much time the following day as they could training to be militiamen. A couple of State Troopers were waiting to get started.

The equipment they were given was a bit of a hodgepodge. All four of them received .40 caliber Smith and Wessons. The individual weapons were a variety of different models and ages taken from the State Police stock of spares and retired weapons. They were given instructions on firing, cleaning, and maintaining their new weapons. Tom was comfortable with all of it. Horst was far less comfortable and turned out to be a bad enough shot that for a while some consideration was given to replacing him. Fortunately by the end of the day he was making progress. Tom was nowhere near as good with his weapon as their police trainers, but they seemed pleased with his abilities.

The other thing they were lectured on and practiced was how to handle bad situations and how to work as a team. Great emphasis was placed on avoiding confrontations and how to retreat safely. It was drilled into them that they were not cops and that running away from a conflict was a really good option. Horst was clearly on board with that, and Tom embraced the idea that his top priorities were to scout building sites and get back to Elaine, not in that order.

The next day the Governor came and spent an hour rubbing elbows and shaking hands. He then proceeded to speak to the small crowd about the survey project. Finally he swore in four of the first militiamen in Vermont's new force. He pinned newly-made Vermont Militia badges on their shirts. Shortly afterward he was on his way to his next stop and the four new militiamen headed back for more work with their trainers.

By the end of the day, Horst was settling down pretty well with his gun and the State Police trainers finally relaxed. They finished the day adjusting the trainees' holsters and belts so they would work for both walking and biking.

Bill and Jill were hosting the bon voyage party for the north survey team. Besides eating and visiting, Tom and Horst worked on loading up their bikes. They had a full camping setup just in case, but expectations were that they would be sleeping indoors in comfort. Many places where they would be welcome to spend the night had been identified, and they were authorized to find a motel if they needed to. They also carried a small amount of food, but again the plan was for them to buy prepared food as they traveled and to have a nice sit down dinner every night. They were told that although they should not waste money, the important things were to get the job done well, and, if possible, quickly.

Early the next morning they were on their way. An hour later they were met in Fairlee at the bridge by a State Police trooper and a planner serving the region. The planner was a mild mannered man who knew the area well and was reasonably well versed in the emerging planning requirements for radically efficient communities. He mostly deferred to Horst about how practical it would be to build on the high ridge opposite the bridge, but managed to offer some useful insights.

The trooper could not have been more different. She was a tough, hard-headed military veteran who loved the high ground on the far side of Route 91 that looked down on the bridge and thought in terms of pinning down invaders, flanking their forces, and returning them to where they came from, whatever that meant. About two hours convinced Horst and Tom that the preselected site was entirely suitable for their purposes. Since none of them knew of any other nearby sites they thought were nearly as good, Horst and Tom decided to move on after lunch.

The ride to Bradford was easy, and they were the first to arrive. They relaxed for a few minutes until a different state trooper and planner arrived. Unfortunately, this site was not as easy as the Fairlee site. There were some locations near the bridge that were suitable for defense that the trooper liked, and there were sites farther from the river that could house lots of people that the planner liked. They carefully examined those sites and then moved on to a compromise site. It was farther from the river than the trooper really liked, but closer than the one that had more room. It seemed like a decent compromise, but no one especially liked it. They worked for hours trying to sort out a good spot, but at the end of the day – literally – they had not come to a conclusion. They decided to move on.

An hour later they were in Newbury knocking on the door of the place they were planning to spend their first night.

Two days after that they were pedaling into Lower Waterford around noon. As planned, they met their contacts on the corner of Maple Street at the library. The planner, Brad, had brought lunch for everyone, so they sat outside the library to eat.

When everyone had received their sandwich and side dishes, Horst struck up a conversation. "So Brad, this kind of seems like the epicenter of the whole border mess."

"I guess, maybe. It sounds like White River Junction might be just as bad, or nearly so. And of course there are more migrants held up at the Route 91 crossing from Massachusetts than anywhere else."

"Good point. I don't know what the Route 91 crossing and the smaller ones are like. We certainly avoid crossing into New Hampshire any more than we have to. There's an ugly feel to things when we cross back into Vermont. My wife refuses to cross into New Hampshire any more unless she absolutely has to. I mean, crossing into New Hampshire is fine. It's crossing back into Vermont that she hates."

Brad nodded agreement about how unpleasant crossing back into Vermont could be. "For planning, it's sort of interesting that both Lebanon and here have interstate bridges and local bridges crossing the river and each one has a dam nearby. They're all closer together up here, but I'm not sure if that's good or bad.

"One thing's for sure – there's nothing very good about the situation. The bridges are bridges. I feel like bridges are meant to bring people together. Now we're using them to keep people apart. And I worry about people using the dams to cross. Swimming across is even worse. They're both dangerous ways to get into Vermont. And the worst of it may be how people stuck in New Hampshire are getting pretty upset, now that we're running out of summer."

Again Horst responded. "I hear you. At least we're working on doing something about it."

"You guys are from New Thetford, right?"

"Yup."

"That's good stuff you're doing."

"We think so. If we can get some new sites sorted out, we're ready to help get some more construction projects started up – pronto. I just hope to hell things hold together long enough for good things to start happening. It's all turning into a powder keg if you ask me."

They worked hard that afternoon. The trooper wound up only vaguely satisfied about defensive options they worked out for the bridges and unsatisfied about defensive options for the dam. However the other three wound up feeling good about finding a site for a large, radically efficient community to accommodate thousands of climate refugees. For them defensibility just wasn't as important.

Two days later, after a long day of scouting sites, they wearily pedaled into Canaan. That evening Tom brought up an idea he had been mulling over. "Horst, it's been kind of bugging me – I think we may be going around this scouting thing the wrong way."

"Huh. I've been thinking some too – not sure we're doing the right thing. Not exactly anyway. What are you thinking?"

"Well, it just feels wrong talking about defensive emplacements along the New Hampshire border. Sure, there are problems we need to solve, but if we're really serious about solving the important problems, we need to be really careful about how we spend our energy." Tom scowled as he thought about the implications of defensive emplacements.

"Yeah. It just doesn't feel right to be thinking about defending ourselves against New Hampshire. Against climate refugees. Hell, most places you could swim across the river. Lots of people do that now, I guess. They must be pretty desperate."

"Uh huh. I suppose in the short term some kind of control may be necessary, but what we need now is capacity to absorb refugees. Hell, they're people ferchristsakes! Housing, agricultural capacity, basic services – that's what's going to get us through all this. That's where we need to focus."

Horst nodded agreement. "And New Thetford has a lot of that right. And your Nousamont project too. We need to put people where it's easy to get food, water, and shelter for starters and then build on that. That creates more friends and allies – people building Vermont up – and gives hope to people who are still stuck at the border."

Tom continued. "Exactly. So here in the valley there's plenty of water and some good building sites. What we need to figure out is how to put as many people in one spot as possible to reduce infrastructure, but small enough overall that they can operate the farms around them efficiently. Just the basic stuff about how to create a new REC."

Horst added, "Along the river here, the big thing that varies is how wide the flat farmland along the river is."

"And we need to keep the walk times to remote fields down. In fact walk times should be pretty much the same everywhere." Tom's scowl eased as they sorted through their ideas.

"Which means that what changes is the sizes of the towns that can be created." Horst grew animated as they put their ideas together.

"Yeah, that's it. You got it. And we don't even need to be exact. If the plan is for something a little smaller than should be possible, they can change the plan and make the town bigger."

"And if they build something that's too big, they can maybe clear some more land. Or shrink the community and re-use the building materials somewhere else since it's mostly all so standardized."

"Yeah." The look on Tom's face showed his satisfaction.

They thought a minute, before Tom added, "We're doing well with our survey work. We should finish up tomorrow, and we could be back to New Thetford in three days, probably. But maybe we could do another plan – a second one – on the way back."

Horst rolled along, building on Tom's idea. "We could check our conclusions on what we've already done like we already planned to, but the second plan could just modify any defensive positions depending on any new ideas we have and then add more community locations in stretches where it's a long way between bridges."

"Yeah."

They talked for a while before settling in for sleep, but they were happy with what they were onto with their new ideas.

The next day they took care of the Canaan and Beecher's Falls crossings and then returned to the previous night's lodging in Canaan. They were both excited to be on their way home.

Over the following days as they moved homeward, they identified three additional promising locations for new communities to fill in long stretches where nothing was planned yet. It wasn't a huge addition, but it was maybe enough for another ten thousand refugees, which seemed like a good number of people to convert from refugees (who could become problems), to new settlers who were part of a solution they believed in – a way forward that brought more hope to more people.

Another realization was that they didn't need to limit the number of settlements near crossings to just one. When the realization struck Horst and he explained it to Tom, Tom's response was to smack himself on the forehead with the heel of his palm. "Jeez! I'm such a dumbass. If we do that we can really increase the number of extra refugees we can accommodate."

Horst laughed. "Tom, you're a lot of things, but a dumbass is not one of them. And I'm sure you would have thought of it too."

"Whatever. I'm just really glad you did."

Everything went well until they got to Bradford – almost home. They were undecided about pressing on the twelve or so miles more miles to New Thetford and home as they approached Bradford when they thought they heard shots near the bridge. Half a minute later a siren sounded maybe a mile away toward the highway, headed in their direction. Horst called in to the Vermont Militia hot line to see if they knew anything. As they connected to the hot line, a State Police cruiser barreled through the junction just ahead of their position. The Militia dispatcher informed them that the state police were responding to the shots and a report that several men had forced their way across the bridge at Bradford. A trooper had been in the area and was responding. Less than a minute later as Horst talked to the dispatcher, the siren stopped. A flurry of shots immediately followed.

According to their dispatcher the trooper now found himself

under attack from multiple attackers and was requesting assistance urgently. The dispatcher then inquired whether they were in a position to offer assistance. Tom and Horst paused. Then there was another flurry of shots accompanied by a distant cry of pain. Horst looked at Tom, who nodded. "Sure, we'll help."

They hopped on their bikes and turned onto Waits River Road, racing toward the river. They were crossing the train tracks when the state police cruiser came out of some woods, driving backward at a high rate of speed. Four men ran out of the woods, chasing and firing at the police car. Tom headed to the left side of the road and set up behind some stone stairs leading into a feed store. Horst headed to the right and took a position behind a pile of logs in a parking lot. Horst immediately got on the phone to the dispatcher and filled her in. She let the trooper, who was approaching their position, know where the Militiamen were. The trooper stopped his car on the right shoulder, between the two of them. Tom got on his phone as well. The dispatcher relayed a message from the trooper that he would try again to get the intruders to stop. If they advanced on his position as he expected they would, Tom's and Horst's job was to protect him from the sides.

The attackers continued moving forward and in about a minute were getting close. The moment the trooper got on his PA and ordered them to surrender, all four started shooting at him. They spread down along the sides of the road using trees and other cover and kept moving up. They were getting pretty close when the trooper called to the dispatcher to pass on that the militiamen should start shooting.

Tom's first shot missed the guy he was shooting at, but hit a tree next to the guy's face. He screamed, grabbed his face and went down. Barely a second later, Horst fired at one of the men on his side of the street. The first few shots missed, but the fourth shot found its target. The man went straight to the ground, as if he were boneless. Distracted by the attack from the sides, the other man on Tom's side strayed from his cover. As Tom and the intruder were taking aim at each other, a shot rang out from the trooper. The man went down.

The last man, seeing his friends on the ground, injured or dead, raised his hands. The trooper took charge of restraining him while Tom and Horst kept their weapons trained on the men on the ground.

When he was done restraining the attackers, the Trooper motioned for Tom and Horst to join him.

"Thank you. That was very bad. You guys made all the difference." Tom was about to respond but the trooper continued. "I think we may have people hurt on the bridge. It would be a big help if you could see to them while I stay here."

When Tom and Horst agreed to go, the trooper continued. "Be careful. I'm pretty sure these are the only four we need to worry about, but be alert."

Tom and Horst hopped on their bikes and pedaled for all they were worth. When they got close to the bridge, there were a couple of people who looked like they were helping some others who were injured. There were a few others tentatively crossing the bridge, but they stopped when they saw Tom and Horst approaching.

Tom got to the bridge first. Not thinking, he went to a man lying on the ground with a jacket covering his head and shoulders. Tom lifted the jacket. The man's face was a gruesome mess from a gunshot wound. The next thing Tom knew, he was on the ground, wildly disoriented and vomiting violently.

Seconds later Horst was at Tom's side. Horst grimaced as he put the jacket back over the corpse's head, and heaved a heavy sigh. After taking another breath he knelt beside Tom. "Tom, I'm going to see what's going on here and I'll be right back. Take it easy. I got it."

Tom oriented on Horst's voice and worked on figuring out what he had said. His mind whirled and he vomited again.

Two minutes later Horst returned. Tom was now sitting but was unfocused as Horst explained. "There are two others injured. One doesn't look too bad, but I'm worried about the other one. There are some other refugees who came over to help who are taking care of them. I called for medical assistance, and they're on the way." Tom didn't respond – he was still in a bad way. Horst looked him over. "Tom, I should take care of a few things. Just give a shout if you need anything."

It was several minutes before the ambulance arrived. Horst directed them toward the badly injured man and explained about the dead man. More people started showing up, and one of them volunteered to take over for Horst so he could see to Tom. When Horst got to Tom's side, Tom was weeping. Horst comforted him awkwardly. A few minutes later Horst was able to get him on his feet and moving back toward the highway. They walked their bicycles slowly.

Horst made arrangements for a place to stay – it was getting late and Tom needed down time. Horst called people in New Thetford to explain what had happened and when to expect them.

A little later, troopers came around to thank them for their help and to interview them. Horst handled most of it, although Tom was slowly coming out of his funk. Horst had managed to get him to eat something. It wasn't much but it seemed to help. Shortly after the troopers left, Tom fell asleep. He slept badly.

Despite being short on sleep, in the morning Tom was much better. He wanted to simply get on their bikes and head home. Horst got him to sit down for breakfast. Again, Tom didn't eat much, but when he finished a small plate of french toast, Horst was satisfied. When he went to pay, the cashier refused. "Your money's no good here guys. We heard what you did – how you helped out, and about your trip up the river. I'm grateful and I know a lot of others around here are too. You have a good ride home."

The ride to New Thetford was leisurely. Tom was still drained. Truth be told, Horst was feeling much the same. The man he had shot had died. He didn't tell Tom since he was still hurting, but it was a heavy burden for Horst. With each of them struggling with his own inner turmoil, it took them almost two hours.

There was a small reception committee camped out at the side of the road, waiting for their arrival. Greetings and welcome homes were brief. Soon Horst was heading home with his wife and Tom was going with Elaine. Once home, Elaine and Tom lay beside one another in bed and Tom told her his stories. As he talked with her, he unwound. He struggled as he told her about the previous day's fight, but felt a little more at ease after he had. Before long he was asleep again. He was feeling much better when he awoke two hours later.

Just before lunch, Tom took a walk and checked in with Sean about work. Sean told him to take whatever time he needed. More than anything else Tom wanted things to be normal, but figured he should get some things from his trip sorted out. He headed home again, checking in with Horst on the phone as he walked. They agreed to get together after lunch to start organizing their report.

As he and Elaine were preparing lunch, Tom got a call from Horst. One of the people who had organized the whole survey effort was going to be coming down later that day to get their initial feedback. "I figure the two of us can get stuff mostly sorted out by the time he gets here. Better to get this trip behind us sooner rather than later if we can." Tom agreed wholeheartedly.

Over lunch, Elaine filled Tom in on goings on in the greater Thetford area during his trip. Tom was quiet, happy to listen to small talk. After lunch, Tom headed to Horst's apartment to work on their notes in preparation for the official visit later on.

When Tom got to Horst's apartment, it was pretty clear that Horst was feeling his own after effects from the previous day. He was haggard and unfocused, and when Horst explained that the guy he had shot had died, Tom sympathized.

Since Tom was recovering better, he took the lead in organizing and supplementing their notes. Later that afternoon the official came by and Tom laid out their thoughts and explained their notes. With some input from Horst, they expanded on their thoughts about making rapid settlement a priority. As they explained, they both became more animated, their belief in what they were proposing serving as an antidote to the hard events of the previous day.

As they were finishing up, the official expressed his appreciation for everything they had done. Then he explained that State Police officials had mentioned about the fight and the trauma Tom had suffered, and passed on contact information for counselors in case either of them felt that it might be helpful to talk to someone. Finally, as he was leaving he once again earnestly thanked them.

Chapter 27

Tom got back into the swing of things at work over the following week. He and Horst had attracted some notice for their thoughts about how to manage things at the border. When the other team returned a couple of days later they liked the suggestions from Tom and Horst about the importance of focusing effort on resettling refugees and between them figured out some additional sites to consider for settlements. Like Horst and Tom, they hated the idea of working on defending Vermont's borders.

Following the survey trips, things seemed to ramp up quickly. Both Tom and Horst did take up the offer from the State Police for some counseling. Tom wound up feeling it was a good thing. The whole thing still troubled him, but the councilor's perspectives really did help. Horst expressed much the same opinion about his own experience with the counselor.

Chapter 28

It didn't take long for the results of the crossings survey results to work their way through Vermont's bureaucracy, and not long after that both New Hampshire and Maine announced they were coming on board with expediting the resettlement of climate refugees, drawing on the insights gathered in Vermont. Massachusetts was slower to do so, but did indicate they were positively inclined towards Vermont's ideas. States elsewhere were also expressing interest. Sean was put on notice that most of his workers who were willing to work on other projects would be relocated in the near future. He was promised good, experienced construction people to replace them – people who could come up to speed quickly with the help of the experienced people who would remain in New Thetford.

The other thing that took up some extra time was the Vermont Militia. Although the militia wasn't large, the state was making a push to expand it. It seemed like there was some kind of Militia-related training or recruitment event every week, and at every event, Tom saw new faces. The word was that the rate of recruitment was increasing, which confirmed Tom's own impression.

The hierarchy within the Militia was still taking shape. Based on his age and experience, Horst had agreed to take on the leadership of the local group, and Tom found he had some status as well based on his experience and the incident in Bradford.

The other big news was that incidents on the border were increasing in frequency. The one that Tom and Horst had responded to was the worst one yet, but violent encounters at the border were becoming common. The incidents made it crystal clear to everyone that people were tired of being stuck in refugee camps for months, and were now sick with worry over the approaching winter. The only thing that helped stem the growing strains was the recruitment of construction professionals from among the refugees. It introduced real hope that they too might have a future – something they could look forward to. Waiting was still hard, but even glimmers of hope that better days lay ahead helped alleviate the fear of some refugees.

Out of the blue one day it struck Tom that his father might be a great fit for a senior slot in New Thetford. Carter's dad, Cam Johnson had just recently arrived in New Thetford to work with the farming crews and the word was that it was going great, so during their lunch break he called his dad to suggest it.

"Tom, thank you for thinking of me. I'm happy that things are going well for you. It sounds really interesting. And it's so good to hear your voice."

There was something about his father's words that didn't feel exactly right, "Dad, you sound a little off or something. Is everything OK?"

"You know Tom, your mom and I should come up for a visit. We can talk more details when we get there."

Tom poked and prodded some more, but that was pretty much all he got.

When Tom and Elaine called that evening to work out the details of a visit the following weekend, the planning went fine, but Tom's mother was just as close-mouthed as his father had been. At the end of the call, Tom was worried.

Sean was happy to hear that Cole would be coming and might be recruited to work on the New Thetford project. Tom had often talked about his father and how good a carpenter and contractor he was, and Sean had come to have faith in Tom's judgment. He figured that if the father was anything like his son, he could hardly go wrong.

Over the course of the week, the situation in Lebanon, NH got worse. A group of people from the southern coast of Virginia had shown up a few weeks before in a school bus and were making trouble about being held up in their effort to get to Canada. To make it worse, they appeared to be attracting a growing group of supporters. The situation had become very tense. Officials from both Vermont and New Hampshire had circulated, trying to calm people. However before long they thought better of it, given some of the responses their efforts at peacemaking drew.

All of which left Tom worried about problems at the border for his parents until Sean made special arrangements to facilitate their crossing into Vermont. It helped ease Tom's concern, if only a little.

Saturday came and his parents arrived at around 10:30 in the morning – just a little later than expected. When they drove up in the big-ass truck at Bill and Jill's, Tom's spirits lifted, thrilled to see his parents. Tom found it odd that he was also happy to see the truck – a vehicle that over the years had almost become Tom's sibling. Tom wondered a bit when he saw that the big-ass truck was full with a heavy load of tools – the same kind of stuff they used on the New Thetford job site.

When his parents had gotten out and stretched after their long ride, Cole explained that some protesters were getting aggressive as some cars were let through while others weren't. "It got a little tense there. We looked like refugees with our truckload of stuff. We drew some nasty looks from a few of the protesters when we pretty much sailed through. But just before we got to the bridge, we noticed a school bus that seemed like the center of a lot of activity. They were hauling steel plates inside and removing the front window next to the driver. None of it looked good to me."

Soon the conversation turned to other matters. As Cole started, Grace took his hand in hers.

"So Tom. And you, Elaine, and Jill and Bill. A little over a week ago, Grace and I got some bad news. It turns out that a little cough I couldn't seem to shake wasn't what I thought. They did some tests. It's cancer."

Tom was shaken. It had never occurred to him that his father could ever be anything but healthy and strong. A cold or a stomach bug sure, but cancer seemed unthinkable. He still looked fine, but cancer was a big, scary thing.

As Tom gathered his wits, Jill asked in a quiet voice. "Cole, what else did the doctors say."

Fear flickered across Cole's face. "It's lung cancer. It's bad."

A shocked silence descended. Elaine took Tom's arm and huddled against him. Grace hugged Cole. "How bad is it Dad?" Tom's voice was choked with emotion.

"It's bad. The doctors said they might be able to do some treatments, but the chances are slim to none that it would do any good. And the chances are slim to none that I could even get 'em. Everything is scarce these days, and fancy medical treatments are just about the worst."

They talked for a little while, but before long Cole broke the gloom. "We had to tell you all this and we wanted to do it in person. We've done that. Now I want to take a walk and see what you are all so excited about here. I saw some of it when we were here after your post graduation adventure, but I want to see it all. To tell you the truth, I could use a break from all this cancer crap."

Bill and Jill stayed behind to finish setting up lunch and explained it would be waiting whenever the others finished their walk. As they headed out, Cole grabbed a small backpack from the truck.

Tom and Elaine led the way, showing them the construction project that was now approaching the top of Cobble Hill. Tom showed his dad the simple modular framing system that worked so well. Cole was intrigued. He liked what he saw. It was clear he was enjoying it.

As they got up several floors, Elaine showed them through their little apartment. Grace complimented Elaine on the work she had done to turn it into a home and they chatted briefly about a couple of ideas Elaine was considering. As they were leaving Cole lingered behind to use their bathroom. Although no one noticed, when Cole caught up, his backpack was less full than it had been.

They proceeded up to the hilltop to where they could look out over the river and the existing farms and new farming projects that were a key part of the New Thetford community project.

"Tom, this is wonderful. You weren't kidding about that." Cole was smiling, happy.

Grace took her turn. "Elaine, I love your apartment. I love what you've done with it. At least I figure it was you." Grace looked skeptically at Tom, who rolled his eyes and looked away. "Just like I thought. You are your father's son, and your father doesn't have a clue about home decorating either." She smiled up at Cole as she took his arm while he gazed across the farm fields arrayed below. It was an image that came to Tom's mind countless times in later years. He wrapped his arm around Elaine.

Cole returned his attention to Tom and Elaine. "You kids have grown up so much. So fast. It isn't fair. You should have had more time to just be young. But we're so proud of you. Both."

They talked some more, but it wasn't long before they headed back to Jill and Bill's to share a meal with loved ones.

As they were finishing lunch, Tom's phone rang. He listened intently, saying little. But the look on Tom's face and the little the others overheard was disturbing.

Tom hung up and looked at everyone around the table, his eyes wide. "The Militia is being called up."

There was a shocked silence.

"That old yellow school bus you saw as you were crossing the river. You were right about those steel plates – they armored it. They mounted what a trooper recognized as a .30 caliber machine gun." Tom looked at his father. "A SAW."

Cole translated. "A squad automatic weapon. That's a serious weapon."

"Yeah. They pushed through the barriers at the border. When border people tried to stop them, the people in the bus cleared the way with a couple of bursts from the SAW – killed a bunch of people. As soon as they crossed the river they jumped down onto Route 5 and headed north. They say that the word is they're headed this way to take over New Thetford. The state is calling up the Militia, but so far here in New Thetford that's me and Horst and a few others. Maybe a few dozen or so. There's a big crowd following the bus and lots of them have guns."

"Tom, you can't go!" Elaine was upset and afraid.

"I have to. I don't want to, but I promised I would." Tom paused. "They said to put together as many people and guns as we can and to muster up at the quarries south of Quail John Road."

Cole Grady quietly took charge. "So Bill, do you have a gun?"

"A deer rifle. A 30 ought 6."

"Are you in?"

Bill paused. "Yeah, I'm in. I hope I don't shit my knickers."

"You may have lots of company today if you do. Tom, let's go out and unload my truck. It might be useful for hauling things today. But the tools should be useful around here."

Cole and Tom headed for the truck, and Elaine, Grace, and Jill followed. They set to work unloading the big-ass truck. A minute later Bill hurried up, his rifle in hand and a backpack on his back with a couple of boxes of cartridges slopping around in it, to join them in unloading.

In short order the truck had been emptied, its contents forming a heap in Bill and Jill's side yard. Another deer rifle and a shotgun that had been part of the load now lay on the tailgate of the truck.

"Dad, what about the drums by the cab?" indicating what looked like fifty five gallon drums secured at the front of the bed under a tarp.

"Leave 'em there. They might be useful." Cole surveyed the yard. "I think we're as ready as we're gunna be. Hop in. Bill, you wanna drive?"

"Sure."

"Tom, honey, why don't you hop in the back?" All three men stopped and looked at Grace as she picked up Cole's deer rifle from the bumper.

"Grace, what are you doing?"

"Going to fight beside my son and my husband. I know how to handle a gun. You taught me. What are you doing?"

There was a pause. "OK, let's go."

Elaine and Jill stepped forward too. This time Bill intervened. "Jill, I know you're willing, but I know that you don't know about guns and you don't have one. Elaine, I'm guessing the same is true about you too. Tell you what though. There could be a lot of people in need of medical attention later today. You might save a lot of lives if you organized that."

Jill shrank back a little, struggling with the realities she faced. But when she looked up, the determined expression on her face told the story. She nodded to Bill, and turned to Elaine. "Elaine, I could use some help."

Agonized over the realities she faced, Elaine looked at Tom. Then, eyes brimming with tears, she turned and went with her aunt.

Tom hopped in the back and Bill climbed behind the wheel. He turned south on Route 5 and headed for the quarries. Along the way, they picked up several other armed men and women headed their way.

As they drove, Cole worked to absorb the lay of the land, asking Bill a question here and there. At Quail John Road they pulled over and let their passengers off.

Cole turned to his wife. "Grace, I'm working on understanding how we might fight this battle today. Maybe someone else will be in charge, but I figure that with my experience in the Army, the more I know, the more help I can be. I need Bill to drive, if he's willing, and I may need to ask Tom to do some scouting. I think we need someone here to organize things so we can deploy quickly and efficiently. Would you be willing to take that on? If there's someone else doing that, fine, but see if you can't help them. You're good at organizing and we're gonna need it."

Grace considered for a long moment. "I'll do it on one condition." Cole waited attentively. "Actually two conditions – that none of you do anything stupid, and that you all come back safely."

"Well lots of folks would say running toward a fight is stupid, but apart from that, I promise to use every ounce of smarts God gave me. And coming back to you is the whole point – of my life really. That's the best I got."

Grace gave him a hard look and kissed him. He slid out of the truck to let her out. Tom jumped out of the truck's bed to receive his hug and kiss, and then slid into the cab, followed by Cole. Bill put the truck in gear and drove south.

"How far we going, Cole?"

"We need to figure out where they are and how fast they're moving. If you see any sign of a school bus coming our way or a bunch of people with guns, stop and get ready to get us the hell out of there."

Bill drove while Cole rubbernecked. Tom held out a map for his father to refer to and answered questions when he could.

As they drove they encountered an increasing number of cars full of people headed north with lots of guns visible. A few places along the way they could look across a field and see a few small groups of people and some individuals hurrying toward the quarries. Bill seemed unconcerned and waved to a number of the people they saw, which confirmed to Cole and Tom that he was confident they were on their way to join the Militia that was forming. They drove on.

At the corner of Route 132 there was a State Police cruiser, lights flashing. A trooper stood beside it. She motioned for Bill to stop.

"Sir, please turn around and return the way you came."

Cole leaned across and responded. "Officer, this is Tom Grady, a sworn member of the Vermont Militia. He has recruited his uncle, Bill Freeman" nodding at Bill, "and me. I'm Tom's dad, Cole."

The trooper looked at Tom and recognition showed on her face. Speaking to Tom she said, "Pleased to meet you Mr. Grady. Mr. Freeman. Mr. Grady. I'm Sergeant Grant."

"Guys, Sergeant Grant is our commander at this point. Sergeant Grant, I was in the service for ten years. Army. Infantry. I separated as a Master Sergeant after service in the Arabian Peninsula. What I really was was a First Sergeant – I ran a combat platoon until I got kicked upstairs for awhile. We saw a lot of action. My son can handle himself and is a good runner. Bill is a good man and knows the area. How can we help?"

Sergeant Grant's response made it clear that she was happy to have their help, especially Cole's. It took them a minute to sort things out. Cole gave Grant the latest on the muster in the quarries. Grant informed them that the front of the intruding force was about a mile away and they were moving toward them at about two miles per hour, maybe a little faster. It was led by the school bus Cole had seen. The right front window had been removed and the .30 caliber SAW was mounted on the hood in front of that. There was another cruiser, driven by Trooper Abby Chan, ghosting their formation from the front. The big question seemed to be the size of the opposing force.

Cole summarized their situation with an idea. "Sergeant Grant, I would suggest that you have us work on determining the size of the opposing force, then. Maybe have Tom scout their western flank."

She thought for a moment. "I think you're right about our next step. And like you say, I appear to be in command. If you're willing, I would like us to form the command team here. That said, I also think it's time to drop the whole rank thing. Please call me Lillian. Okay if I call you Cole?"

With first names shared, Lillian continued. "Trooper Chan – Abby – is young and very fit. She's good. How about we have her go with Tom on foot to scout their column. We'll have Bill take her cruiser and keep an eye on their lead element. And maybe be close by in case our scouts need help."

Lillian called Abby to come back and swap Bill into her car and get things organized for their scouting mission. While they waited they worked out the initial details of a plan.

Abby arrived a minute later. She shook the Militiamen's hands and showed Bill how to use the radio. Before Abby, Tom, and Bill headed back south, Lillian took a moment. "Now Bill, remember, we can replace or fix the cruiser and anything in it except for you three. Be safe."

Bill nodded and headed south, moving out smartly. Cole's heart caught in his chest at the thought he might be sending his son into battle, and was amazed at the idea that his son, brother in law, and a young trooper now compromised the forward element of a still-forming militia.

Word came over the radio that Horst had been recruited to get some other volunteers to the Route 132 overpass over the big highway to keep an eye on the intruding force as it passed on the road at the bottom of the slope below them, and also to try to defend the bridge if it came down to it. The idea was to keep the main body of intruders contained on Route 5 if they could.

With things starting to come together on a defense, Lillian and Cole headed north in their vehicles to work on arranging the main defense. As Cole headed back up the road they had just come down, he started to develop a clearer appreciation of the lay of the land. Along this portion, Route 5 ran on the flats beside the river. The land between the road and the river varied in width and elevation, none of it being particularly wide and all of it being fairly low. From Cole's perspective, the western side of the road was more interesting, being higher and possessing more of the kinds features that might be useful in a fight – especially trees and berms to hide and shelter behind. As they drove they passed two more troopers in cruisers heading south to take up position at the intersection of Routes 5 and 132 to help with communication and to organize and support action from that direction.

As they were pulling into the main base of operations in the northern quarry, Lillian got the bad news from Abby over the radio. She and Tom had found a good vantage point to view the advancing column and estimated that the main body of intruders was over a half mile long. Over most of that length people were densely packed, which, when they did the math, worked out that there were somewhere around five thousand people in the column. Their initial assessment was that well less than half of these were armed and they were poorly organized – a rabble, not an invading military force, when Abby explained it.

Although the number of invaders was daunting, the news about poor organization and lack of firearms was a relief, especially to Cole who knew how much training, discipline, and logistics mattered in a fighting force.

Radio traffic confirmed that state police units were streaming in from around the state with additions from Sheriff's departments and local police forces in the region, which would be a huge help in command and communication. However, their numbers were tiny. The Militia would have to provide the backbone of the resistance.

Now that Lillian and Cole had a decent picture of the situation, their strategy quickly emerged. They planned on lining the western flank of the intruding force with snipers – which meant anyone with relevant military experience and a good hunting rifle, or experienced hunters who were willing to shoot people. Each sniper would be at the center of a squad comprised of a runner, whose job was to maintain communications along the line, and armed people to defend their position and the sniper. Ideally each squad would be commanded by a sworn member of the Militia or a police officer. Otherwise they would just have to sort it out as best they could.

When Lillian and Cole got to discussing deployment of their people into the hills and fields overlooking Route 5, Lillian mostly just listened to Cole. Although she had some appreciation for the value of the high ground comprising the invaders' western flank, it was Cole who knew tactics and had a much deeper appreciation of troop deployments.

When she had first arrived at the north quarry, Grace had joined a group of people working to organize things and together they had done a decent job collecting and sorting out resources, which pretty much meant people and guns. They were now tasked with organizing squads, with the goal of having sixty squads – one every fifty feet – to cover a flank of about three thousand feet. It was a start.

As the squads formed, Cole and Lillian went through and talked with any who were ready. Lillian explained their mission. "What we need to do if we can is to stop the intruders' column in order to protect New Thetford. Our first priority is to degrade the command and control elements of the intruders – which means the snipers are to shoot their leaders in order to sow confusion. The job of the other people in the squads is to protect the squad. You are *not* to shoot anyone not engaged in hostile activity. Is that understood?" Lillian's instructions were accompanied by a fierce glare that instilled the fear of God into people on this point.

With this point driven home, Cole took over and reviewed the priorities. "Like Sergeant Grant said, your primary targets are anyone trying to organize other people. As long as we are fighting a rabble, we have a key advantage." He did not add that given the lopsided numbers, they needed any edge they could get. "The second priority is to shoot anyone firing a weapon or looking like they're going to, and to shoot anyone attacking you or a nearby squad." As an afterthought Cole added, "If you find yourself looking for more targets, shoot out the engines of vehicles in the intruders' column. That passes a message to them without hurting anyone. Other than that, no shooting."

Someone came by with a box full of rolls of colored duct tape for arm bands, hat bands, or other markings to distinguish friends from foes. Lillian thanked her and set her to work, happy that their motley force was pulling together.

At that point word came back from Abby Chan. She and Tom had finished scouting the flank of the intruders without incident, and as they headed back north, they had joined Horst at the overpass. They confirmed with greater confidence that the main body of the intruding force was a half mile long, was a rabble, not an organized force, and numbered approximately five thousand people. They also observed that people were deserting the column in fairly significant numbers.

Cole silently gave thanks that his son was safe, and was pleased to hear about the desertions.

One of the troopers tasked with supporting the Route 132 overpass force gave the scouts a ride up the highway and let them off at the closest point to the quarry headquarters so they wouldn't have as far to run.

New Militia recruits were flowing in at a good clip, which was a very good thing. Based on what Grace and other organizers said, they were coming up on a thousand Militia. Even combined with approximately fifty police units, this was not a good number compared with the five thousand of the opposing force, but with their own numbers growing quickly and the numbers of the opposing force shrinking as people deserted, Lillian and Cole felt OK. What gave Cole the most hope was the good organization and arming of the Militia, at least when compared to the intruders. It sounded like the Militia already had almost as many guns as the opposing force and most of the incoming recruits were reasonably well armed.

Lillian and Cole agreed it was time to start deploying their squads. At that point Tom and Abby trotted up, lightly winded but ready. Before Lillian sent Abby to head up the most remote team and assist in deploying squads along the way, Cole spent a minute explaining the importance of good cover to Abby – for hiding before the fight started and for protection once it did.

Before the squads moved out, Lillian and Cole once again double teamed them to drive home their mission – to sow confusion among the enemy ranks and protect themselves and nearby squads, with the goal of halting the intruding column's progress before it broke into open ground leading to New Thetford. Again they stressed that anyone who did not pose an immediate threat was not to be shot.

When the first sixty squads had been sent on their way, they still had almost as many left, with an average of about twelve people per squad. To Cole, these numbers seemed pretty good. Lillian was less confident, but it was what they had. It was certainly impressive under the circumstances. The new squads were tasked with filling the gaps between the squads that were already deployed, wherever they could find good cover. By the time another sixty squads had been deployed there were a fair number more squads assembled. They were tasked with either joining existing squads or filling gaps as best they could.

Grace was serving as the sniper with the squad assigned to the top of the rise on Quail John Road. Cole now assigned Tom to join them as a runner. Then he and Lillian moved into the roles they had assigned themselves for the coming engagement. Lillian was to confront the advancing column alone in a final effort to end the intrusion as peacefully as possible. Cole admired her courage, but did not envy her in the least. Cole's job was to wait in his truck close by at the top of Quail John Road to serve as mobile reserve, which meant to travel to wherever he was needed most and haul anything that was needed elsewhere. They drove slowly out of the assembly area up to Quail John Road. Cole pulled over where Grace's squad was positioned in a protected spot. As Lillian drove by, Cole snapped a salute to her. Lillian calmly saluted back, made her way down to Route 5, and turned right to face the advancing column. She positioned herself close to cover – a line of farm equipment – in case the need for it arose. Lillian sat for a moment. Then she got out of her cruiser and moved around to the front. She stood there, feet spread and arms crossed over her chest and waited.

The school bus leading the column continued forward toward Lillian. When it reached the edge of the barn about a hundred feet from her, Lillian flexed her knees to be ready to move if needed, and then lifted her hand, indicating they should stop.

Their response came a second later. Seeing activity behind the machine gun that was pointing her way, Lillian sprinted toward cover and dove. A stream of bullets started at the driver's side of the cruiser, shredding it, and chased her toward the tractor she had dived behind. Lillian scrambled forward on her hands and knees to put as much distance as possible between herself and the long burst of .30 caliber rounds chasing her. It mostly worked – no bullets struck her, although flying glass and debris drew blood.

Back at the top of the hill Cole couldn't see exactly what was happening, but by the sound he knew it was bad. "Fuck." He motioned for Grace and Tom to join him. Another trooper sitting nearby listened.

"Shock and awe. Like in Kuwait. That's what we need now. Be ready to pour it on when the bus clears the house down on the road. Take your positions." Cole nodded pointedly to the trooper in the cruiser to make sure he had understood. The trooper acknowledged with a nod.

Cole could tell by the sound and reflections in the windows in the barn across Route 5 that the bus would be coming into view any moment. "Grace. Tom." They were at the edge of the road, and turned. "Know that I love you both more than I ever thought possible. Now and forever." Then Cole jammed the big-ass truck into gear and hit the gas. All six tires spun, throwing up dirt and rocks from the road. As the school bus appeared around the edge of a garage near the corner, Cole took a small propane torch, its flame already burning and held it out the window, driving one handed. The big-ass truck accelerated rapidly down Quail John Road toward the bus.

The big-ass truck impacted the school bus just behind the driver's seat. It's speed and mass were almost enough to knock the bus onto its side, but not quite. However the barrels of gasoline and lube oil still tied securely at the front of the load bed were the main show. They ruptured, spraying highly combustible liquids over the bus.

Just before the impact, Cole had flipped the propane torch up. When the spray from a ruptured gasoline barrel touched its flame, a massive fireball bloomed, enveloping the bus.

Meanwhile at the top of the hill Tom was shocked as his father sped down the hill. He and Grace started walking down the hill. As the nose of the bus appeared beyond the edge of the house, Tom erupted, charging down the hill, his father's shotgun in hand, screaming.

Grace started to follow him but forced herself to stop and think. Knowing she couldn't keep up with him, she prepared to give her son cover fire from where she was.

Simultaneously the state trooper at the top of Quail John Road who suddenly found himself in charge issued an order over his radio. "Attack!"

In the seconds before Cole and the big-ass truck took out the bus, rifle fire broke out along the line and rapidly grew. Seeing and hearing Tom as he ran down the hill, more Militia joined in. As more fighters from down the line joined, a wave of attackers grew into an assault on the flank of the intruding force.

Some snipers could not bring themselves to shoot other people, much as Lillian and Cole had expected. Instead they went after the engines of the cars in the invading column. However most of the snipers quickly took down leaders and anyone with weapons who were responding aggressively. This process was largely completed in a matter of seconds. They then they added their fire to the snipers who were already targeting vehicles. Together they made short work of the mechanized elements of the invasion.

Within the column people saw their leaders dropping dead in front of their eyes and cars getting shot up. The message was reinforced as anyone who was preparing to shoot at the snipers or screaming Militia dropped dead, usually without ever having fired a shot. In less than a minute the invasion became a rout.

Grace ended the life of the school bus driver less than a second before her husband's life ended. Its driver was the luckiest person on the bus that day.

The encounter was very brief. As screaming Vermonters drew near, the intruders' column broke and ran.

Most of the people in the column dropped everything and ran away from the mayhem toward the river. A small number of people who had held onto their guns took up firing positions on the far side of a railroad bed on the way to the river. They didn't get off many rounds before they were eliminated by snipers or advancing Militia.

Crossing the train tracks hot on the heels of those who fled, Tom shot three people who had chosen to continue the fight.

When the following wave of Militia rolled across the bank, Tom turned and continued his pursuit of the main body of the opposition. Behind him, some of the Militia mopped up the resistance at the railroad tracks while most of them joined Tom's pursuit of the opposition toward the river. Once there, a few of the fleeing people jumped into the river and swam, but most of them huddled on the bank, terrified.

Tom was the first to reach the river bank. Adrenaline still pumped through his veins. Fortunately for everyone, the first people he saw were a young brother and sister, huddled together and crying in terror at the sight of him. The sight of frightened children doused the fire burning in Tom. He stopped and engaged his most important weapon, just as his father had instructed. Although alert for trouble, Tom took a moment to think.

Tom lowered his shotgun, holding it ready just in case.

"You are prisoners of the Vermont State Militia. Surrender peacefully and we won't hurt you. I promise." Delivered in Tom's loudest, most forceful voice, it worked. It was probably not the most eloquent demand for surrender ever delivered, but in later years as others discussed the battle, most people agreed the 'I promise' was probably a good touch that helped move things in the right direction.

As other militia members arrived at the river bank, they too stopped and gave their own versions of instructions to surrender. A wave of stillness swept southward along the river.

When the Militia had taken the railroad tracks and the people fighting from behind it stopped shooting, all gunfire had tailed off quickly. The snipers remembered their instructions and held their fire. A few times a shot would ring out. If it came from the direction of the river, dozens of rifle scopes went in search of its source, and the swarming Militia advanced on the location. Such encounters were brief. The few deaths and most of the serious casualties the Militia suffered took place as the Militia assaulted the railroad embankment. By the end of that minute, all firing stopped, marking the end of the engagement.

While others issued their own instructions to surrender and the rate of gunfire rapidly declined, Tom carefully descended the bank to the river and helped the young boy and girl huddled there get back up the bank. Back on top of the bank he helped others as they scrambled up. Other militia followed Tom's lead, and other prisoners followed the lead of the two children with Tom.

There had been a great many twisted ankles and cuts from the headlong flight and pursuit to the river. There were also a fair number of more serious injuries, including many broken legs, ankles and a few wrists – the results of thousands of people running across uneven ground. When the gunfire had abruptly diminished, a medical relief team started out from New Thetford, led by a Sheriff's cruiser, which was followed by a fire truck and a row of minivans and pickup trucks loaded with people and medical supplies. Every vehicle was adorned with some form of a red cross. The medical team, which included Jill and Elaine, was comprised of people desperate to give aid to their friends and loved ones, and looking to help anyone who needed it.

When the fire truck arrived it set to work extinguishing the still-burning school bus wreck and a nearby garage, and knocking down the part of the fire that was threatening the barn on the river side of the road. The medical team set to work aiding the injured. Additional medical teams were sent in as they were assembled.

As Tom made his way back from the river toward the road with his prisoners, his mother made her way to him. When they met, the prisoners waited patiently while their captors hugged and cried. Although they didn't understand the loss their captors had suffered, most of them were touched and relieved by the humanity of what they saw.

By the time Tom's group got to the road, the fire truck had the fire under control. When Tom stepped up onto the road, he heard his name.

"Tom!"

Elaine was running to him. Tom managed to stay where he was since no one had come to relieve him of his prisoners, which did not prevent more tears and hugs when Elaine threw herself into his arms. The embrace wasn't long – they both had responsibilities to see to – but Elaine's face no longer exuded fear when she rejoined the medical teams spreading through the battle site, searching for the injured and giving aid.

A sense of order slowly spread over the scene as more police arrived and took over from the Militia. Minor injuries were treated on site and those suffering more serious injuries were taken to nearby hospitals. Doctors at those hospitals set more broken bones – mostly legs and ankles – in that one day than most did in a normal year.

About a half hour after Elaine and the first medical teams had arrived, a newly-arrived trooper supported by a small team of fresh militia started taking custody of prisoners and moving them back down the road toward the school buses that had been requisitioned to return them to New Hampshire. Tom had been relieved.

Barely a minute later as Tom stood considering his next move, Lillian came over. "Hi Tom." Lillian was limping. Numerous bloodstains showed on her uniform and several bandages provided evidence of her close brush with death.

Tom nodded in response.

"Tom, you are free to go or stay. Whatever you feel is best. You've done fine work today. I appreciate it. But you've done enough." She choked up. "Your dad was a hero. He saved a lot of lives – on both sides."

Tom broke down and cried. Lillian hugged and comforted Tom, and Tom clung to her. After a minute Tom quieted and then stepped back. "Dad had cancer. It was bad."

"Ah, that helps me make sense of it. It doesn't change the fact he was a hero."

Tom cast his eyes downward and nodded.

Lillian waited a bit. "Are you going to be OK Tom?"

"I guess. I guess. He made his death count. That's something."

"Think about how he gave a bunch of other people on both sides of this shit show their lives. The bad guys mostly all died and the good guys mostly all lived. Without him, that would have been very different."

"I guess I see that."

"That's probably all we can hope for just now. Hang tough Tom. I should probably see to some other stuff, but if you'd like we can stay in touch."

"Yeah, that'd be good. Thanks."

As she left, Tom thought for a second. Then he turned and started searching for Elaine. When he found her, they worked together giving aid and comfort to injured and frightened people in need of help.

That evening when Tom and Elaine returned to their apartment, there was a package on their kitchen table. The label said 'To Tom, from Dad." When Tom opened it, he found his father's 1911-style .45 pistol. Raw emotion swept through Tom. Tom understood his father's intention – that he should inherit a treasured possession from his father – but there was much more. This pistol was a symbol of so many things, both good and bad, and it was now his. Elaine stood silently at Tom's side as he opened his father's gift. When Tom sat down at the table, staring at it, she bent over and gave him a gentle kiss on his neck. She left him sitting, pondering, while she went to make dinner.

Chapter 29

Things were crazy over the next couple of days. The news media showed up in droves. They desperately wanted to talk to Tom and Grace, but got no help from anyone in cornering them. Quite the opposite. For camouflage, Tom took to wearing a crusty, colorful baseball cap and was now sporting a reasonably healthy facsimile of a beard. Once in a while a media team would show up in Tom's vicinity and ask for him. One time, Tom looked on as a person working nearby responded to a request by a media crew looking for Tom by pointing at him and proclaiming in the most disingenuous voice she could muster that "Tom is over there." With hat and beard, filthy from the day's work and wearing a foolish look he had quickly assumed, the media crew responded by turning away and leaving, frustrated by another failed attempt to corral a hero of the engagement. Over the years it became one of Tom's favorite stories to retell.

Although it felt like forever, things did calm down. Tom was mostly able to get back to work without distractions. He found that, again, the counseling sessions offered to the people who had been involved in the violence helped.

Grace stayed with Jill and Bill as she grieved. Things weren't good – the grieving was hard – but both Grace and Tom, as well as Elaine, Jill and others who had known Cole took comfort from what everyone agreed had been a life well spent.

The middle of the following week while Tom was at work,

Lillian called. After exchanging greetings she inquired, "So Tom, how are you and your mom doing."

"I guess we'll be OK. The whole thing still doesn't feel real, but I think I'm sorting it out, and I feel like Mom is too. It's just that there's this big hole where Dad used to be." The emotion in Tom's voice was strong.

Lillian paused before continuing. "I can only imagine. I only knew Cole for a short time, and I feel his loss. He made a real impression on me. I remember Bill driving up with you and Cole like it just happened, and the way Cole rose to the challenge we faced. I don't have words for what his help meant to me. Your dad was a very special man. We'll all miss him."

"Uh, yeah." There was a pause on the line. Lillian waited patiently for Tom to continue. "Yeah, I will too."

There was another pause before Lillian continued, "Well, I was in the neighborhood and I was wondering if I could get some of your time. There's an interesting idea I'd like to run by you."

Tom cleared his throat. "I'd have to check with Sean, but I'd be happy to."

"I already talked to him. He's fine with it."

"OK then. Where do you want to meet?"

"I'm in Sean's office."

"OK."

There was a pause that struck Lillian as a bit odd. Then the door opened and Tom walked in. "I was in the neighborhood."

Lillian smiled. Tom was hard not to like, and her admiration for him was strong. Based on the events of the terrible day when they met, she felt a certain kind of closeness with him. A special kind of trust. "I've been wanting to see this place. Maybe we could walk, and talk?"

"Sure thing." They headed out.

Lillian got right to it. "Tom, I'm sorry to say I don't have as much time as I would like today. I was happy to hear that you're getting along. Your mom too. I wish I had some special ideas – some kind of wisdom to help, but I don't. As bad as that day was, you have lots of friends and people who love you. When bad things happen, that's about as good as it gets, sorry to say."

"Thanks. How about you? You're doing OK?"

"I guess. I get some bad dreams about the bus coming at me. The psychologist says that's OK. It'll get better. That's the worst of it."

"I guess that's good."

"I guess. Anyway, there's something interesting I would like to talk over with you."

"What's that?"

"Things are happening fast. Some powerful people have let it be known that they want things moving in a good way – a good direction – that prevents anything like that day from ever happening again. Abby had an idea I wanted to check with a few other people first, before I ran it up the flagpole."

"OK."

"Abby thought that recruiting climate refugees into the Vermont Militia might be a good way to choose which ones get into Vermont first, along with the people working on all the new construction projects. If they get through some training and handle themselves well, we nudge them up the list. Try to find spots for them. Jobs. Whatever. It isn't perfect, but other than specific skills or something like that, it seemed like a good idea."

Tom thought for a long minute. Lillian looked around as they strolled through some of the better-established bits of New Thetford. She really liked the feel of the place now that it was emerging from the chaos of construction. There were a few people on the walkways – enough so that you could imagine how it would feel as it became a bustling community, which would be soon now given how quickly things were moving. The great thing was that there were no cars. It felt quiet and safe and human. It felt good.

"That seems pretty good – a pretty good idea. It gives people here more reason to interact with them in a good way. Get to know them some. It won't be perfect, but it's something."

"Uh huh. I think maybe that's the biggest thing. And some people like to join and be part of something bigger. That works for me too."

"OK, I guess I'll have to take your word on that, but it makes sense. Anything that gets them moving forward, toward something. Not stuck. With some hope, and not so afraid."

"Yeah. I like that. There's also the part that you may not like –

it makes the Vermont Militia bigger. Sometimes numbers like that matter. The other big thing I like is the whole second amendment thing. Some people think it means that they can own any gun they want and do most anything they want with it. Having a big militia means we can drive home the very first words of the second amendment – about 'A well-regulated militia'. Some people like to forget about the well-regulated part of that. This gives us a chance to remind them."

"It's sad that it could come down to having a bigger militia. But like they say, sometimes it's better to have it and not need it than need it and not have it. But mostly I don't want to think about shit like that. Please pardon the language. Anyway, I like what you say about the second amendment. Taking up arms, bearing arms, should be well-regulated. If they had been, my dad would still be alive. Some other good people too."

Again, Lillian gave it a minute. They walked on. "Well, that's pretty much it for the big question. Thanks for your thoughts. I was hoping it made sense to you. It means a lot to me that it does."

Tom nodded. They walked for another minute. Lillian was again impressed that New Thetford felt like a good place to be, but was also struck by a somber feeling. She realized it could have just been a reflection of how she and Tom had both been injured by the events of the terrible day they had shared. In her head she figured that things would get better, but her heart was still heavy and she simply knew that Tom was feeling much the same.

"I wish I could stay. I'm glad I could at least see a little of what's going on here. I like what you're doing, all of you. In times like these, the road can be rough. Places like this. People like you. You help with the rough patches."

"You too Lillian. You too."

They smiled at each other. "I guess I should be going. My best to your mom. Elaine. Bill. All of you guys." She gave Tom a hug, and he returned it.

"Stop by again. Try to leave some more time. We'd love to show you around the whole place. Spend some time."

"This is a great place, Tom. I'll definitely be back."

Chapter 30

The earlier drive to move forward with an aggressive program of creating radically efficient communities had been getting bogged down in political maneuvering until Vermont's governor made a unilateral decision to stop waiting on others and to do the right thing with or without others' support. The rumor was that his favorite phrase these days was 'Just do it.' As this was happening a semblance of normalcy slowly returned in New Thetford. However as the Governor's initiative gathered momentum, New Thetford experienced a new kind of disruption from the departures of a large fraction of the construction workers there and the arrival of their replacements, mostly drawn from climate refugee camps in Vermont up on the Canadian border, and in New Hampshire and Massachusetts on Vermont's borders.

The media loved the story of the changes in Vermont, and every network ran stories about it every day. As it turned out, Americans loved it too and gave it their enthusiastic support. It wasn't long before the Governor, as it seemed was a fairly common thing among Vermont politicians, was said to be eying a run for the White House. The whole thing became so popular that it wasn't long before Vermont was hard put to spend the money that was flowing in. The governor made a point of sharing part of the excess money with programs outside of Vermont, which drew some criticism, but boosted his overall popularity even more.

As Lillian had hinted at, people at every level of the government suddenly became very serious about massive resettlement. Precipitated by the dramatic events in Vermont and boosted by the Governor's initiative, people now accepted that things were different – there was no going back to the way things were. A consensus that best way forward was to get people settled and productive as soon as humanly possible emerged and quickly grew strong, and, surprising though it seemed, policy quickly followed. The situation certainly wasn't good, but it was improving quickly.

Both New Hampshire and Maine, as well as half the other states bordering Canada were quick to follow Vermont's lead. Radically efficient communities were embraced as the foundation of the change that was needed. New Thetford became the primary model for how to do it and the main pool of talent for creating new RECs. People, especially the best and the brightest, flowed through the New Thetford construction project quickly and then fanned out to projects throughout New

England and increasingly to other northern areas of the US.

Over the following months and years, they were joined by construction workers and other construction professionals from around the world, looking for fixes to similar problems in their countries.

Chapter 31

Three weeks after the battle, Sean called Tom and Elaine to his office.

"Tom. Elaine. Something has come up. Something that from Vermont's perspective is very good. I'm not sure how you'll feel about it, but I guess there's only one way to find out.

"The province of Quebec has agreed to ratchet up admitting climate refugees in a big way if we'll help. And to put it bluntly, in this case 'we' includes 'you' – both of you." Tom and Elaine glanced at each other as Sean continued.

"You are part of the group they want to lead the effort. Frankly they don't have a lot of trust in the US government – things at that level still haven't recovered from past problems. Things are much better with the state of Vermont, but what it boils down to is they are entirely willing to do this given help that they trust, and you two are high on the list of the Americans they trust."

Tom and Elaine again looked at each other, taken aback. Tom

was much quieter since the battle, so Elaine responded. "So by 'us', you really mean Tom."

"No, not really. Well, yes and no. They like you a lot Elaine. No question that Tom has a higher profile, but you have a reputation of your own. People like you, and people who know you know how smart you are. People who know you are also impressed that you're a natural leader. There's no denying that Tom is the one people think of first, but they want you both very much."

"And what is it they want us to do?"

"They want you there to help build Nousamont."

That got their attention. Tom interjected. "Do you know what that means? Exactly?"

"Exactly? No I don't. What I think it means is write your own ticket, within reason."

Tom and Elaine talked to each other for a minute before responding to Sean. "Can we get back to you when we've had some time to think?"

"Absolutely, Elaine. People are hopping up and down they want this to happen so bad, but I am entirely happy to tell them to fuck themselves – nicely of course – for as long as I have to. You two have done enough for others to last a lifetime. Whatever you want is what's going to happen as far as I'm concerned."

Tom interjected again, "Would it be OK if my mom came too, if she wants to."

"The issue hasn't been brought up, but I just can't imagine it would be a problem. Should I ask?"

"No, not yet."

"OK. So, take whatever time you need to sort this out. Whatever happens and whatever you decide, you have my support."

Tom and Elaine decided to take the day. On the way over to Jill and Bill's house they started to grapple with this new twist in their lives. They both liked New Thetford a lot, but they were both deeply troubled by the violence that had been part of their experience there. They yearned to put it behind them. As they talked, the question for them became how best to do that.

They were both tremendously happy about the commitments to RECs that had now been adopted so widely and enthusiastically. They both also agreed that although the things happening in Vermont, New Hampshire, Maine, and other northern states were good, the big story was Canada, just like Team Carbon had decided so long ago. It was farther north and therefore had better prospects in the more distant future. But mostly, there was a whole lot of land that was getting better and better as a place for people to live as the Earth continued to heat up, as opposed to most of the US where, in most places, things were going in very bad directions.

They found Grace lingering over coffee at Bill and Jill's. They joined her and explained what was up with them. They asked her what she was thinking about her future and whether she might want to go to Canada too if they went.

Grace was slow to respond. "Well, that's an interesting

question. One thing I *have* decided about my future is that it isn't going to be in Newburyport. I'll miss people there, sure, but it isn't the same town it used to be. That plus I'm not the same woman I used to be. Wherever I wind up, I'll be facing a lot of change, and without your dad, or you and Elaine presumably, it isn't the place where I want to start over again.

"I like it here. Jill and Bill have been wonderful and I like the people here. I don't know what I would do here, but I guess that's the same regardless of where I wind up. But I could live here.

"Canada is interesting. I guess the whole area up there is pretty remote, but it sounds like that's going to change pretty fast. And nobody knows what living in a full-blown radically efficient community is going to be like, no matter where it is.

"Then there's the mess we've made of dealing with climate change in the US. Canada isn't perfect. Far from it really, but it seems a lot better than here, what with all the deniers here who have made things so much worse – have hurt so many good people."

She paused and had another sip of coffee, and then another.

"Road trip. We should have a road trip so you can see it again. I would love to see it too. Maybe we should have a road trip."

Everyone loved the idea of a road trip.

On the way back to talk to Sean, they ran into Carter and told him what was up. He got excited and started asking questions. After responding to a few, Elaine laughed. "This is like déjà vu – like when we talked to you about coming here."

Tom smiled at the memory, and Carter laughed. "Yeah, you're right. Got any room in your car?"

Elaine glanced at Tom. Their ESP was working just fine. "We just might."

"OK, now I know I'm pushing it – what about my dad?"

"Huh. I bet we could work it out. Not Mace?"

"Well, no. Things between us weren't going in a good direction before the whole thing with the Militia – the battle. Afterward things between us fell apart completely. It just like stopped. Now Mace has hooked up with another guy. I'm happy for him, I guess."

"Tell you what. We're on our way over to talk to Sean about this stuff now. We'll clue him that there might be a couple of others interested too. You talk to your dad and we'll check in with each other tonight."

It was agreed, and they continued on their way.

When Elaine laid it out for him, Sean liked the idea of a road trip. "That's a great idea. Let me know what I can do to help."

"Actually it was Grace's idea. Would it be OK for her to come too?"

"Sure. Absolutely!"

"Carter is interested and he thinks his dad might be too. We think there might be a few others too."

At that point, Sean got a faraway look in his eye for a second, and then smiled. "Yeah, why don't we think in those terms."

That evening Tom, Elaine, Grace, Carter and Cam got together at Bill and Jill's to talk things over. Cam was the most enthusiastic one about moving to Canada. "Carter and I have been bouncing around for too long. I want to be settled. I like it here, but I think the area north of Amos may be more like North Dakota than here, which might be nice. But I can't really say why – I just like the idea of it. Too bad my French is so rusty."

Then Jill jumped in. "I don't know about Bill, but I would love a road trip. See the place where people I love just might wind up."

Bill added, "If it's OK, I'd love to come. Maybe we can make it a cultural exchange – it would be really good to build connections with what they're doing."

They talked for awhile, but it was still early when they called it a night.

First thing in the morning Elaine and Tom checked back in with Sean. The more Elaine explained, the more Sean smiled. When she was done, Sean responded. "A cultural exchange. I think Billy hit the nail on the head with that one. I've got about a dozen people eager to go see what's happening up there. And you know what? The Canadians have about two dozen people who want to come down and see our operation. I'm liking this a lot."

By the end of the day, things were basically set up. That Friday, a bus from Canada would show up with somewhere around thirty people on board who wanted to see New Thetford. There would be a community party that night for them to meet everyone and to spend time with the crew that would head north on Sunday. On Saturday, the two crews would spend most of the day touring around New Thetford together. On Sunday morning, the New Thetford crew of not quite thirty people would board the same bus, joined by three of the Canadians who came for the weekend. That evening when they arrived in Amos there would be a welcome party. The Americans would spend the following week working together with the Canadian crew in Amos that was gathering together there to build the new community while the Canadians visiting New Thetford would work with the American crews to collect insights on how to do it right. The following Saturday, the Americans would hop on the bus and return to New Thetford, and the Canadian crew would head home on Sunday morning.

In no time the whole New Thetford community was abuzz about the cultural exchange/road trip. They were excited to be sharing what they were doing with what was getting started in Canada. Although no one said it, the fact was people in New Thetford had been tightly focused and working hard for a long time and were kind of in a rut. Even more than that, there had been a pall over the community since the battle. Almost no one anywhere questioned the necessity of what the Militia had done, but no one who had fought felt good about the whole thing. It had taken a heavy toll on morale.

This event did a great thing – it took people's minds off the terrible things that had happened and turned their minds to a good and hopeful sharing with like-minded people. New Thetford would never be quite the same after people's experiences around the battle, but the anticipation of the visit was a balm to people who were deeply shaken by that day's terrible events.

Chapter 32

That Friday night was one hell of a party. Afterward, the joke was that if you could remember the party, all it proved was that you weren't there.

Saturday morning started late. Thanks to their greater resilience, the younger contingents of both crews were only a little late to get moving, although one of the older Canadians, Pierre, did make it and even managed to be vivacious. The others joined up with them over the course of the morning as they toured New Thetford, starting with the core area where many people were now living, through the areas where construction was still in progress, moving on to the surrounding farm fields, and ending up with a foray into the woods that surrounded the fields to see the agroforestry and animal migration corridor projects underway there. As they walked, Elaine noticed that Pierre could often be seen in conversation with Sean and a number of the most senior people walking with them.

After the tour was finished, they all joined together for a happy hour. Thanks to a large number of hangovers from the night before, very little alcohol was consumed. A working dinner followed. People just talked to each other about everything anyone could think of – about things the Canadians had seen earlier in the day, about things Americans would be seeing in the coming week, to bat around ideas people wanted to try out on an interested audience – anything that people wanted to talk about. And again, Elaine noticed that Pierre seemed to be the center of a great deal of attention from the most senior people.

In the morning, the Canadians met the American crew at breakfast and spent time with them until eight, when they all headed out to the bus. As people boarded, the Canadians who were remaining in New Thetford wished them all a good trip. After the bus got on the highway, many of the passengers set about catching up on lost sleep.

Shortly before they crossed into Canada through Derby, VT, Pierre, who was returning with them to Amos, came by to collect passports. As Tom passed his passport to Pierre, Tom thought briefly of Hiro collecting passports from a bunch of high schoolers as they were about to head into Canada from the other side of Vermont, so long ago.

When they stopped at the Canadian border, Pierre greeted the customs officials and accompanied them inside. It wasn't long before they returned and Pierre rejoined the people on the bus. From the spot beside the bus driver, he thanked the officials who had come outside with him. One of them, an older woman whose uniform was little fancier than those of the others responded in French. Elaine and Tom were sitting near the front of the bus and Elaine, who had been working on her French, perked up at what she heard.

After Pierre had returned to his seat and they were pulling out from the station, Elaine leaned over to Ted, another of the Canadians, who happened to be sitting across from them, and asked "Ted, did that customs official address Pierre as 'Deputy Premier'?"

"Ah, Elaine, your French is getting good. The answer to your question is 'oui'. Our government is taking this effort very seriously and wanted to make sure we had the best person possible to move things forward. The premier wanted very badly to come, but was afraid that his position would interfere with the kind of communication we wanted to have happen. And since Pierre was even more excited than Jacques, the Premier was willing to step aside."

As Ted reorganized himself in his seat, Elaine and Tom looked at each other, eyes wide.

At the request of the Americans, the bus made a brief stop at the restaurant that was the site of the tornado incident a year earlier. Elaine and Tom were ambivalent about the stop, feeling like the tornado had marked the beginning of a very hard time. And although she wanted to see it, Grace was unsettled as she was able to better understand the near miss Tom and Elaine had experienced. She appreciated the support offered by Cam and Carter as they walked around the parking lot together. Although neither of them had been involved directly, father and son both shared many of Grace's feelings about their friends' experience.

The welcome for the Americans in Amos was cordial. By the time they arrived, the cat was out of the bag about Pierre. As a result, it was less of a surprise when their friend of a few days, the second most senior member of the Quebec's executive branch, introduced each of the Americans to Jacques Fortier, the Premier of Quebec. The premier turned out to be very well informed and very excited about the effort, and was buoyant as he welcomed the visitors from Vermont.

The dinner that followed was pleasant, although the mood was different from the Vermonters' welcome to the Canadian crew. Canada had suffered from many climate change-related problems, but not the way people from New Thetford, and especially the way New Thetford's Newburyport transplants, had. The Canadians' mood was a combination of eagerness to get started and awe over their guests' expertise with radical efficiency and their dramatic experiences. Everyone enjoyed themselves and discussions were productive. It was only an hour or two late when things broke up for the evening with everyone sharing one thought – they were all eager to get to work the next day.

The enthusiasm was even stronger in the morning. Focused, detailed discussion started at breakfast and essentially continued non-stop all week long. As long as at least two people were awake, chances were they were engaged in deep and detailed talk about the initiative.

The first morning's formal agenda started with an introductory meeting, after which they all headed out to the site. It had been renamed from Nousamont to Alamont (for 'to the mountain') in deference to the sensibilities of French speakers. Elaine, Carter and Tom all liked it. The excitement was palpable as they piled out and hiked up the rise to the proposed building site – the same knoll that had been selected by Team Carbon a lifetime ago. Most people clustered around Horst as he carefully examined the site and shared his thoughts.

As Horst talked with most of the team, Tom and Carter decided to have a run up to the peak of the mountain. They were joined by other runners. When they got to the top of Mont Douamont and looked all around, a full three hundred and sixty degrees, they were awed by the glory of the new day's glowing, clear light. Although they didn't linger long – they all wanted to get back and get to work – it remained a moment that those who made the run would always treasure.

The rest of the week was a get up early and work until late in the evening affair. Elaine, Carter and Tom had never worked harder or loved it more. Late Friday afternoon – the last full day of the road trip – the entire group convened for a final meeting. Various committees reported about what they had done and plans that had been made. Through it the feeling of rightness about what they were doing grew and took on a clearer form and greater substance.

After the final report had concluded, Elaine raised her hand. "I wanted to share some thoughts from discussions that Tom and I have taken part in this week.

"I think it may have been Pierre who first used the term 'climate haven' early this week to describe what we are building at Alamont. At New Thetford we always talked about what we were building as radically efficient. And of course what we built is radically efficient, but when you think about it, radical efficiency was a means to an end. The end point – the goal – of all that effort was to create a climate haven.

"We feel like making this distinction between means and ends is important. When we do, it kind of frees us up to think a little differently about what we're doing. Of course we can also think of climate havens themselves as means to an end – the goal being to reverse climate change while preserving a safe, secure, and comfortable lifestyle until we're done fixing the mess we have made of the atmosphere.

"We were talking about this last night and then got to a slightly different idea – that as great as climate havens are for helping get people through climate change, there may be places where we want to have people live for other reasons. It seems to us like there are places that make them bad places for most people to live but are still worth the extra effort needed to establish and maintain them – places like seasonal settlements for winter pasturing, or mobile camps to support ecosystem restoration. Places like these could be really helpful in addressing problems climate havens face but can't fix for themselves.

"After we talked about it for awhile, Tom had the idea of calling places like this climate bastions – places that are worth the extra effort despite hostile climate conditions or other big challenges. Talking about bastions instead of havens for places like these might help us think better about how to create and use them. I'm especially interested in climate bastions for ecosystem restoration, especially for planting programs for enhancing the water/rain cycle to use this effect to cool the earth. I know Tom thinks more about things like maintaining transportation networks and finding feedstocks for biochar manufacturing, which are great too. Anyway, I just wanted to share our thoughts on this stuff."

When Elaine finished a buzz of low conversation started and a bunch of hands went up. A discussion got started and would have continued, but Pierre nudged the talk back to the meeting's agenda. However when the agenda was completed and the meeting was breaking up, many discussions about climate havens and bastions started, including one between Pierre and his boss, Jacques Fortier, who had given himself permission to show up for the wrap up events despite concerns about any chilling effect of the presence of a powerful politician on proceedings.

"That Elaine Inoue is a very bright young woman. Everyone talks so much about Tom and all he has done. And of course he has done impressive things. But I think maybe we are very fortunate that Elaine is part of all this as well." Pierre couldn't have agreed more.

That evening Tom and Elaine disappeared after dinner. At one point Grace wondered where they were, but before too long they were back.

What no one knew at the time was they had disappeared to talk about something Pierre had brought up with them early that week and they had discussed with him several times since. Elaine and Tom had decided they needed to talk it over – just the two of them. When Friday evening rolled around, it was kind of 'now or never'. They took the opportunity to return to the little park on the shore of the Harricana River where they had shared their first kiss.

At the park they made their way to the same bench and wrapped themselves in a blanket borrowed from their room. They got things started with a re-enactment of the big event from a year or so ago. The kiss was just as sweet as their first one, so long ago. When they were done, Elaine asked, "So, what do you think?"

"I think the kiss was wonderful, you're wonderful, and I love you."

"Tom Grady, you have a one track mind and you're incorrigible. And I'm a very happy girl and I am crazy about you too. But we do have something to talk over."

"I guess. OK. What I think is that this has been a great week, and I didn't see how it could get any better. But it did. I like it. A lot."

"Me too. I did want to go to college. I think we made the right decision to not go last fall, in spite of the hard things that have happened to you. It's been wonderful this week to see you so happy. Big boy." Tom was amazed by how Elaine's crazy sexy voice was still getting better.

"You know, babe – we're going to have a lot of work over the next five, maybe six years if we do this new college thing."

"As long as it's with you, I'm going to be happy."

"Yeah, that about says it for me too." The kiss that followed sealed the deal nicely.

"What are you going to study?"

"Civil engineering, just like I was going to do at UMass. What about you?"

"Soil science. Microbiology. Soil ecology. I want to get really good at growing great soil."

"You're going to be great at it."

"You're going to be a great engineer, too."

"I'll be fine, but I'm not smart the way you are. I think I'll probably have to settle for 'good.' But I'm fine with that. Maybe someday I'll do project management. But I'm really a one step at a time guy. Some day maybe I'll work my way into management stuff, but I have a lot of work to do before then. Meanwhile it blows me away how smart you."

"You too Tom."

"I'll do fine. But academically you're in a different league. You're going to shine. You're going to do great things."

"But no pressure." Elaine smiled, and Tom's heart melted for the millionth time.

"I really like the whole work/study thing. It's sort of like what we were doing in the New Thetford apprenticeship thing, but with coursework added in. I think my dad would have liked the idea of me having a degree. He still would have called me a dumbass when I screwed up, though."

Elaine didn't respond immediately. When Tom looked at her, trepidation showed on her face. "Maybe we should have a baby so you have someone to call a dumbass when he screws up."

A new emotion awoke in Tom. The idea of a baby had come up before, but before it had been just words. Now, for the first time, Tom felt something. Not what Elaine was feeling, judging by the look on her face, but suddenly he could imagine something more than just the two of them. He wrapped his arms around her, pulled her close and gently kissed her forehead.

"Maybe someday we will. But this time I'm the one who isn't

ready. We have to finish school, and things – climate problems – have to at least start turning around before I would want to be a father."

Elaine was quiet for a minute. "I guess you're right. It's just that every time you smile at me I get weak in the knees and start thinking about babies."

"Think about soil ecology for now. Healthy soil is a big part about providing for a baby."

"And so is a radically efficient community that's secure and baby friendly."

"I'm on it babe. So, how about we take the blanket back to our room and I find a way to warm you up before we go back with the others."

"Sometimes you have the best ideas."

When they returned to the function room the group had monopolized for the week, Grace pulled them aside. "I think we should talk. You know – about what people are thinking. About plans." Elaine and Tom were agreeable, so Grace corralled Jill and Bill, and Cam and Carter.

Cam was first to weigh in. "I like it. I'm in if Carter is."

"I like it too Dad. What about you guys?" looking at Elaine and Tom.

"Tom and I love it. Grace, what do you think?

"I like it, although my thinking isn't completely settled yet. I guess I'm still reeling a little from everything that's happened. But, I like it. I like the way it feels – it feels right. I'm not ready to say absolutely yet, but I think I may have a new home."

Bill and Jill both loved what they had seen, but planned to stay in New Thetford, at least for the time being.

The conversation started to drift, but Elaine brought it back to the previous topic. "Tom and I wanted to let you know. We're staying. We aren't heading back with you tomorrow. We're happy that Cam and Carter are coming back for sure, and, Grace, we hope you'll come too.

"And while we're making announcements, we have another – Tom and I will be going to college! Tom's studying engineering and I'm doing soil science."

The response was surprise and excitement, combined with some confusion. Elaine cut to the chase. "Canada is starting up a new online-slash-live climate adaptation college program – the Canadian Institute of Radical Efficiency. At least that's what they're calling it for now. Pierre mentioned it to Tom and me earlier this week, but asked us to keep it under wraps. They've been thinking about doing it, but wanted some feedback about New Thetford's apprenticeship program before making it official. There's going to be an official announcement early next week.

"They say they were inspired by the internship program at New Thetford and wanted to build on it. I guess one of the things they wanted to do was talk to Tom and me since we were some of the first people to get into the New Theford program.

"They want the program to be decentralized – dispersed to places that already have expertise, including lots of RECs.

They figure it'll help them get it going quickly and help keep it real. In fact they say that almost all the professors will work on building new RECs. They're actually going to get their hands dirty.

"Alamont will be the site of the primary Canadian campus. It'll be small – 2000 students or maybe fewer. Vermont is going to be part of it too. The location for the primary campus in Vermont is undecided, but they're hoping to locate it between Fairlee and Bradford, on top of a hill overlooking Lake Morey, on its west side. The thinking is that two of its academic specialties would be agroforestry and managing agricultural operations in hilly terrain.

"All of the course material will be shared online – free for everyone – and they're going to use the latest content management tools to slice and dice the content for as many audiences as they can. Horst is going to lead the framing systems program and maybe some site survey stuff. There'll be several places working on regenerative farming techniques because of how different they can be, you know, depending on local conditions. Alamont will be one of those.

"Besides the regular academic program there's going to be a certificate program for experienced construction professionals and others for farmers and foresters. They're going to be based here at Alamont, at least for now. They say the construction program could move around a lot since construction here will tail off before too long and they want that program to be associated with active construction projects."

"Me too! How do I enroll?" To the surprise of no one who knew him, Carter was excited about it too.

"Hey, you know, they didn't tell us that. We'll let you know. You let us know if you find out first." Everyone laughed.

Grace was excited too. "Sounds like Alamont and Fairlee are going to be the first radically efficient college towns. It sounds wonderful."

People talked until late, ignoring the need to get up early the next morning. As things were finally breaking up, Grace took a moment with Tom and Elaine. "OK, you got me. I'm in. I'll be back as soon as I can." Elaine squealed and hugged Grace. Tom skipped the squealing, but his hug was just as heartfelt. "It's so wonderful – you two going to college. I want to be part of that and everything going on here. I can't wait to get back. But right now, I need to get some sleep. If I can."

Chapter 33

The following morning people straggled into the lobby of the hotel. The demand for coffee was high. The buzz of conversation was muted, but happy. The undercurrent of excitement was strong, the more so since things were moving forward so quickly. When the bus started loading up, the goodbyes were happy ones. The week at Alamont had reignited excitement and hope in those who had suffered through the hardships in New Thetford.

Carter almost decided to stay too, but in the end wanted to say goodbye to New Thetford. He, his dad and Grace would be back in two weeks, more or less, anyway. They just needed to take care of a few things in New Thetford and go to Newburyport to get things moving to conclusions there. Grace summed it up when she said, "I can't wait to get back here, to our new home."

As people boarded the bus, once again hugs were shared and kisses bestowed. It was an odd feeling for Tom and Elaine when the bus doors closed, and another as it pulled away. They waved to the people on the bus, who waved back until they couldn't see each other. Tom and Elaine watched until the bus turned a corner and was lost from sight.

As it disappeared, they turned to one another, hands at each other's waists. Their road to this place had been rough – sometimes very rough. But standing together, looking at each other and looking to the future, Tom and Elaine were happy.

"You know, Elaine. I was thinking about what you said yesterday. About a baby."

Elaine was taken aback, and it showed on her face.

"I mean, I still think we need to wait on that, but there is something else we could do."

Tom had her attention. "What did you have in mind?"

"I've been thinking that I want to spend my life becoming the person you need me to be. I was thinking you could marry me." Encouraged by the look on Elaine's face, Tom took her hands in his and lowered himself to one knee. "Elaine, I love you and I want to spend my life with you. Will you marry me?"

Elaine's face flushed and joy suffused her smile. She lifted on their joined hands and Tom rose in response. "Tom, I want to always be the person you need me to be. I love you and want to spend my life with you. I will marry you."

They sealed their agreement with a kiss.

Epilogue

Many years have now passed since Tom and Elaine waved goodbye to the bus as it returned to New Thetford. As planned, Carter, Grace, and Cam soon returned. Work on Alamont picked up rapidly. Elaine, Tom, and Carter enrolled in CIRE and again distinguished themselves – Elaine for her brilliant work with new methods for quantifying improvements in biological services associated with ecological succession in soils, Tom with his work on helping launch over a hundred new radically efficient communities, and Carter with his knack for solving challenging mechanical problems. Grace and Cam also took courses with CIRE to update old skills and grow in new directions.

Since then, Tom and Carter's work on low-cost, easy-to-operate biochar kilns has helped lower the costs of biochar production. Elaine's work on increasing the resilience and productivity of biochar-enhanced soils has further enhanced the feasibility of scaling up biochar use. Together their work is now considered foundational to the final phases of decarbonizing the atmosphere in a controlled, predictable fashion. It has been a long time coming, but optimism that we are now entering a new age of sustainable prosperity is strong.

Elaine and Tom have come to represent the resilience, intelligence and strength that is allowing humankind to emerge from the greatest challenges and darkest days we have faced in centuries. It has been my privilege to have known them for these many years since that terrible day in New Thetford, and it is with great gratitude and unbounded hope that I dedicate this book to them.

Milo Edwards

THE END

About the Author:

I have been working on the idea of radically efficient communities as an answer to global climate change for seven years now. Along the way I came up with the idea of using fiction as a way to make my ideas more relatable. The result is <u>Rough Road</u>.

About myself – I have always had a strong interest in the environment and in science and technology. I have been an active reader of science fiction, techno thrillers, and other tech-oriented action genres since the ninth grade. Along the way I have written four novels of my own, although <u>Rough Road</u> is the first to be published.

In college (at Marlboro College, RIP) I studied environmental science (focusing on solar energy and energy conservation) and ecology, specifically mathematical ecology. My graduate work (at MIT) was in civil engineering and construction project management.

Along the way I have had diverse experiences. I ran an alternative energy store, taught briefly (and rather poorly, I might add), and worked in Greenpeace as a campaigner in New England and on the (original) Rainbow Warrior. I have done many projects, including designing and building a high-performance, energy-efficient boat, an electric car, and creating a 501(c)3 to assist in the creation of green businesses.

In my semi-retirement, I am actively working on soil health initiatives at the local, state and regional levels, and gardening at my home in St. Albans, VT. My gardening includes research on permaculture and cold composting.

Rough Road

I hope you enjoy <u>Rough Road</u>. I encourage you to contact me with your thoughts and suggestions. I look forward to hearing from you.

Jim (roughroad2020@gmail.com)

9 780578 769240